A Collection of Stories Presented by the

Kindred Writing Collective

the hands we choose to hold

Note from the designer: Hello, my name is Izzy and I like cats.

ISBN: 979-8-9891436-2-7

Printed in the United States of America

Cover design by Izzy Thorpe
Book Design by Izzy Thorpe

authors:

K.I. Runyon

Izzy Thorpe

Amanda Kennedy

Allison Matalone

Christine Urgello

Lee Graham

Tara Henderson

Carisa H-K

Rose Pulford

Brooke Thompson

David Hansen

table of contents

romance

introduction
written by Amanda Kennedy

When you think of human connection, what kind of relationship comes to mind? Is it the familial and life-long connection you have with a sibling or a parent? Our families were the first place we forged connections. We learned to love, fight, and play under one roof with the people whom we first held hands with. These kinds of connections run deep and can be complicated, messy, and enduring. Because they often last a lifetime, they pass through many seasons of life, evolving as we grow and mature.

The romantics among us will say that a look across a crowded room, held just a moment too long, or a fevered embrace is the ultimate connection. There are countless songs, movies, and books to make the case for this. Romantic relationships can bring us to our highest highs and our lowest lows. We feel passion one minute and pain the next, yet we continue to seek it out and extoll its virtues.

In comparison to those connections both romantic and familial, friendship can sometimes appear to be of less significance. Casual and unassuming, friendship can be both common and rare. A friend can be someone with whom you swap book recommendations with and wish happy birthday to once a year on Facebook. They can also be someone who knows where you keep the spoons and whose name and number you put down as your person to call in case of emergency. Our friends are not the people we're connected with since birth, nor are they the ones we find ourselves drawn to in a way that can be described as 'falling.' Our friends are the ones we choose. The people who make us feel seen, heard, and valued. They could even be from whom we derive our strength and sustenance.

It was from a need for this kind of connection that the Kindred Writing Collective was born. In 2019, Tara and Amanda sat at Tara's dining room table, reading aloud passages of Natalie Goldberg's *Writing Down the Bones* to each other and came across this passage:

It's also good to know some local people who are writing and whom you can get together with for mutual support. It is very hard to continue just on your own. I tell my students in a group to get to know each other, to share their work with other people. Don't let it just pile up in notebooks. Let it out. Kill the idea of the lone, suffering artist. We suffer anyway as human beings. Don't make it any harder on yourself.

We looked at each other, and said, "We need a writing group."

In this collection of short stories, poetry, and creative non-fiction, you'll find reflections on the connections we make, the connections we keep, and the connections we leave behind. They all matter, and they all contribute to the richness of our lives. As you sit down to enjoy our second anthology, it is our sincere hope that you feel connected, even momentarily, to the writers within.

friendship

it's just dinner

K.I. Runyon

DISCLAIMER: BRIEF MENTION OF PREGNANCY LOSS

Nat, as her friends liked to call her, waited for Ronnie the doorman to finish fighting against the New York City wind and haul open the big glass door to her building. The man couldn't have been a day less than her seventy-eight years but the tequila from earlier was still weighing her down and so she waited, letting him do the work.

She shivered and tapped the fingers on her right hand alongside her leg while she waited. She'd foregone a jacket today so she could show off her new peony-colored cashmere sweater and the sporty, black pant she'd snagged from Christian Dior's latest line.

The book club ladies would've loved it, but now all she felt was the itchiness of the tag she'd forgotten to remove and the blister on her heel from the flats she'd worn one too many times.

The day had started so well. She'd woken up in time to stop by her favorite coffee shop on the way to her Saturday morning aquatics class. She'd walked in the gym smiling and practically skipping, looking forward to the new music their instructor had added to the class last week.

One of the songs they'd learned to dance to was by some young woman with the same name as that popular witch show in the nineties and it was about one of Nat's favorite things: coffee.

It was after class when things had gone awry. Nat had checked her phone to confirm the time only to find out that her niece, Anna, had postponed their weekly FaceTime to later in the day.

Then, as Nat was walking out, already late to book club because all the hair dryers had been taken, she'd been stopped by Carolyn Myers, who'd gleefully announced the appearance of her fourth great grandbaby.

Nat had smiled and congratulated her with all the enthusiasm of a toddler agreeing to finish their vegetables and then promptly parked her ass at the nearest bar and taken three tequila shots.

The bartender had tried to cut her off after that but she'd cried ageism and he'd had the decency to serve her a few more beers. After missing book club and spending a healthy amount of time feeling sorry for herself, Nat began the journey back to her apartment.

The place had large bay windows overlooking the city and a massive kitchen – by any standards not just New York City – that opened to a living area that'd been furnished by one of the city's premier interior designers. It also boasted four bedrooms.

The only thing the place lacked was people. A widow for eight years now and her husband Robert's name continued to slip past her lips every other time she walked in the door. Even with her cats running around the place, there was never quite the same energy.

Thanking Ronnie and walking through the lobby, Nat used a shaky finger to press the up button on the elevator and stepped back to wait. It took several minutes longer than usual and she wondered if there was a new tenant moving in today, holding things up.

People in this building weren't accustomed to waiting and Nat supposed she was one of them too now. The foyer alone boasted floor to ceiling mirrors, gilded crown molding, and fresh flowers, always. The front desk had not one, but two concierges to ensure the ultimate experience.

Finally, an elevator from the bank on the left dinged and the doors opened. A family of five including a grandfather dressed in formal wear rushed out while the mother yelled at them to hurry. Nat felt the familiar pang in her heart strike again before taking slow measured steps to get on the elevator.

"Here, let me get that," a warm voice said from behind her.

A very tall young man put his hand on the side of the entryway, holding the door open for her. Nat huffed, annoyed that she needed the help, but grateful.

"I'm usually a bit quicker," she said.

Nat took two steps past the guy and situated herself in the back of the elevator. She turned just in time to see the nose on his handsome face wrinkle. He must've smelled the booze.

"Of course," he said, frowning.

He jabbed the button for his floor, the eighteenth, and looked back at her with a question.

"Twenty-two, please," she said, pulling out her key fob and brushing past him to tap it on the access pad.

Not everyone was allowed to go up to the penthouse suite. In fact, in most buildings she would've had her own elevator, but this one was a designated historic landmark and changes were limited.

The man startled a little, no doubt thinking some suave millionaire in his forties would've been the occupant of the top floor. Oh no, quite the opposite.

Shy and kind Robert Clarke hadn't been a Casanova of epic proportions or a man in finance, but he'd worked hard all his life, and about a decade ago when he'd sold the little boutique hotel his family had owned for several generations, he'd earned enough on the sale of the hotel's real estate alone to provide for ten families.

It was too bad that he and Nat had had none. They tried so hard too, but in the end it was just her and Robert. And then poor Robert had had the audacity to drop dead in the middle of supper after three short years of retirement.

Shaking herself of those depressing thoughts, Nat watched the numbers on the digital screen go up, moving too fast to really see them clearly. It made her a little dizzy and if that wasn't a sign of the state of her life, she didn't know what was.

Paragliding in Hawaii and hiking in the Andes Mountains were fun and all, but after a while it all kind of ran together. And none of those things filled her apartment. She huffed, checking her watch.

Before she could read the clock hand, though, a sudden screeching noise rang out and the elevator came to a thudding stop. With the momentum of the jerk, Nat lost her balance and flailed before falling to the side. A hard, warm body caught her before she collided with the wall or the floor, though.

"Oh god," she said.

"Sorry, I didn't want you to fall," he said.

They paused, waiting to see if any other disaster would occur. When it didn't, she responded.

"Thank you. You break a hip at my age, you're done for," she said.

"By that logic, I'd think you wouldn't be drinking at two in the afternoon either," he said. His mouth gaped and then closed. "Sorry, I didn't mean to say that out loud."

She snorted. His judgment wouldn't kill her. She already had a hole the size of Manhattan where her heart was supposed to be. He righted her and stepped back.

The young buck was maybe thirty with soulful brown eyes and beautiful wavy blonde hair that she imagined people paid good money for. He was fit and Nat now knew intimately that he had a six pack. Based on the way his pants contoured to his legs, she doubted the man had ever eaten a carb.

"Are you gonna call 911 or what?" she asked when the man made no move to ring for help.

"Ah yeah, sorry," he said, pulling his phone out.

While she waited, she looked at the screen indicating the floor numbers. It was glitching back and forth between fifteen and sixteen.

Nat rummaged in her purse. She was perfectly capable of calling for help herself, having taken a technology course at a community college a few years back, but why bother when one of those millennials was around to do it for you?

Nat checked her phone while she waited. Her battery was high and she had plenty of time before her favorite show came on but the young man next to her cursed and jammed at his phone screen. Nat looked at hers again and saw no bars.

Of course, the elevator shaft was blocking their service. Nat looked over at the interface where the elevator buttons were and found a bright big red button. She pushed it and it started ringing out loud.

"Hello, my name is Jane. Please announce your emergency," an operator answered.

"Hello Jane, this is Natalya Clarke. I live in the penthouse of Winchester Tower. It appears I find myself stuck in the elevator," she said. "I've also got a young man with me..." she trailed off.

He cleared his throat.

"Micah Sadler," he said.

"Okay, Natalya and Micah, let's see what we can do about getting you out of there quickly," the operator said. "Please standby."

The speaker crackled a bit before it went mute and Nat and Micah were left standing there staring at each other.

"Do you have any water or medications you should be taking while we're in here?" Micah asked.

Nat snorted.

"Calm down son. I go back to my village in Russia every year and it's a four-mile trek from my cabin to the center of town. I walk there *and* back."

"Sorry," he said, blushing. That had to have been the fourth time he'd said it.

"If you say sorry one more time we're going to play the silent game," she said. "Now, help me have a seat."

He assisted her down on the ground so she could lean her head back against the wall. He sat down across from her, one leg extended and another bent, his elbow on top of it, looking much less enthusiastic than before.

"Do *you* have any medications you should be taking?" she asked, getting a small tickling feeling in the back of her brain. He flushed, scratching his neck. "Oh god, you do, don't you?"

"I have type 1 diabetes and I just worked out so..."

"So you're a ticking bomb, is what you're saying?" she asked.

His ears turned red.

"Pretty much," he admitted.

Nat uttered a few curse words in Russian and pulled a half-drunkhalf drank water bottle and some M&M's out of her bag. She tossed the food at him and he caught it.

"I was on my way home to eat lunch. I swear I'm not irresponsible," he explained.

"Whatever. Eat it. I haven't made it this far in life to get my arm gnawed off in an elevator."

Micah ripped open the bag and poured some into his mouth.

"Doid you want some?" he asked around his chewing.

Nat arched a well-maintained brow.

"No, that's all you," she said.

He poured a few more into his mouth. Less than thirty seconds later all the M&M's were gone. Micah crinkled up the wrapper and shoved it in his athletic shorts pocket. She pushed the water bottle forward.

"You're gonna be thirsty now," she said.

He waited for a full ten seconds before he leaned forward and extended his hand to grab it. This time he took three small sips before handing it back. An awkward silence descended and Nat did what she did best – she filled it.

"Have you lived here long?" she asked, studying him.

With his face, he had to be a real heartbreaker. The brown in his eyes was like molten chocolate and the blonde of his hair could only be described as golden. In an odd twist of fate, Micah looked like what she would have pictured a child of hers to look like had she and Robert had any children.

Nat had dark brown hair, well, she had had that, several decades ago, but Robert had had similara skin tone and hair color to this man. Nat also had brown eyes, but again, Robert had been the tall one. Athletic, too. It was strange that fate had taken him and not Nat.

"Just moved in a month ago, actually. With my boyfriend."

"Ah, so you're in that 'I hope I don't fuck this up, but it's my house too' stage?" she asked.

Micah gave her his first real smile and if he was shocked to hear that kind of language from a woman her age, he played it off well.

"Something like that yeah," he said, laughing. "What about you?" he asked.

"Eleven years," she replied.

"Just you?" he asked.

"Just me," she said. *After forty-two years with Robert.*

Micah hesitated and she waved at him.

"Ask," she said.

He gave her a small smile. Where had this kid come from? Despite looking like a cover model, he had the confidence of a rescue dog, curious but hesitant.

"Isn't that lonely?" he asked.

She laughed. It sounded coarse, like sandpaper against untreated wood.

"Why do you think I smell like tequila?" she asked. He had the good sense to duck his head at that but she took pity on him. "Today was an exception. I usually stick with my one glass of red wine at dinner. Despite what they say about us Russians, I realize you can't be slinging back vodka at all hours of the day and not run into any health issues."

He looked back up and nodded. The speaker crackled to life and Micah jumped up, energy levels high for now. He went over to the little speaker to hit the button to respond when the operator came back on.

"Hello, Natalya and Micah, are you there?" Jane asked.

"We're here," Micah said, keeping eye contact with Nat.

"How are you doing? We have maintenance on their way over as we speak. It shouldn't be much longer," she said.

"Yeah, we'll be fine as long as this doesn't take too long," he said.

"Excellent. I'll be back on in ten minutes to alert you of the status of your situation," she said.

The speaker went dead again.

"I'm more concerned about when I need to use the restroom than when I'll get hungry," Nat said while Micah sat back down. Micah checked his watch.

"Well, those M&M's bought us an extra hour or two I'd say," Micah said.

Nat could tell by the slightly green tinge to Micah's skin that they would be lucky if he didn't pass out before half that time. She saw on her watch that twenty minutes had already gone by.

"So tell me about this man of yours," she said, attempting a distraction.

"He's in tech."

"That's nice." He gave her a strange look that disagreed.

"He started his own company five years ago before I met him. Made a ton of money when he sold it two years later. I didn't even know he was wealthy until we'd been dating for almost a year. I was actually kinda mad. Feels weird to live in a building like this. I grew up in a suburb of Ohio and my parents have lived in the same rundown house since I was three years old. I'm a history teacher."

"Honey, my parents' home in Russia didn't have electricity until after I moved out of it and look at me now. Enjoy it." His brows shot up.

"How did you make it happen?" he asked.

"Can't help you there. I was dumb enough to marry for love, but lucky enough that it all worked out. My Robert was a savvy one," she said.

"Where's your husband now?" Micah asked. The levity of the moment disappeared in an instant and she could see that Micah knew he'd stepped on a landmine.

"Dead," she picked at the nonexistent lint on her sweater.

"And uh, you never had kids?" he asked. She sighed, not bothering to look up.

"Life happens. Some things aren't meant to be," she said, skirting the truth.

She refrained from thinking about the piercing pain in her chest that had erupted when Carol had shared her news this morning.

"I can relate to that. If Ryan didn't have money, kids wouldn't be on the table for us."

"You should get a ring on that finger first," she said, changing the subject.

"One day," he said. "Not too soon, though." He winked.

This time when the silence descended it was companionable. Nat pulled her phone out and mentally planned out her meals for the week in her head and put it in her app. When she had service again, she'd schedule her delivery. That was one of this new generation's better ideas.

When she was done about thirty minutes later, she looked over at Micah. He was sweating and kept blinking. It wasn't that warm in here. The air conditioning was about the only thing that was working. He either ran hot or the low blood sugar was kicking in much sooner than he'd anticipated.

"What grade do you teach?" she asked. His eyes lit up despite the glassy sheen to them and he started talking, even if it was less enthusiastic than before.

"Ninth grade. It's the most challenging yet fulfilling one I've ever taught. They're filled with this intense need to belong yet they're over-confident to the point of dangerous. It's fascinating." He chuckled.

"There are so many roads yet to travel at that age," she said.

"There's this one kid, Benjamin." Micah shook his head in exasperation. "Smartest kid I've ever come across but all he cares about is cracking fart jokes and meeting girls. It's infuriating to see that wasted potential but when he's on a roll the entire class is laughing so hard half of them need tissues to clean up their tears afterward."

Micah told story after story about Benjamin's antics to the point where even Nat was laughing, but after the earlier excitement Micah's voice had become less animated and quieter as he went on until he simply stopped talking and leaned his head back.

"Hey, get it together kid. What's Benjamin gonna say if you don't come back tomorrow?"

"Tomorrow's Sunday," came the quiet, sarcastic reply. Nat shook her head and used the elevator railing to hoist herself up so she could press the button.

"Excuse me, Jane? How's it looking there?" The scratching sound of Jane getting ready to reply came through the speaker.

"Any moment now," Jane promised. "How are things?"

"We're going to need you to hurry. We've got someone with low blood sugar in here," Nat said.

"We'll have you out soon, ma'am," Jane said. Nat resisted the urge to say something snarky. She was old, not sickly.

"It's not for me. Micah here is a Type 1 Diabetic."

"What?" Jane's shrieking made Nat wince. "I'll call the paramedics right away. Hang in there," she added. The speaker shut off.

"Ugh," Micah said.

"What?" Nat asked, lowering herself back down. She plopped on the floor a little harder than she intended, having to sit without Micah's help.

"I don't like to tell people."

"Oh, did you feel like dying today?"

"Ha ha. I won't die." Sure, that's why that last word was slurred and he appeared to lack the energy to look up.

"No, you'll just end up in the hospital for a few days. That's much better." Her friend Rosemary's daughter had this same problem so she knew a little bit about it.

Micah didn't respond, but he curled up against the wall of the elevator to lean his head against it and his movements were even slower than before.

The clanking of tools and shouts of workers both above and

below them interrupted what distraction Nat had planned next. From what she could understand from the yelling, there was an object causing obstruction that needed to be removed for the elevator to continue its ascent.

Jane came back on the speaker and informed them that they were going to use the manual override to send the elevator down a few floors so they could get Nat and Micah out before they attempted to remove the obstacle. Unfortunately it would be a little longer. Nat threw the last of the water over to Micah.

"Drink up," she said.

"No, you didn't get any."

"I'm fine. The guilt's gonna hurt worse than the thirst if only one of us makes it out of here," she said.

Micah eyed the water on the ground between them before he made a slow roll forward to grab it and guzzle it down.

"So, do you have any hobbies?" he asked.

She could see it for what it was. An attempt to think about anything but what he was feeling.

"I do waterswim aerobics. I walk, I read. I'm good at crocheting. Keeps the fingers from succumbing to arthritis. And I travel. I visit my nieces and nephew and their families. Most of them live in London. My grandniece just started medical school."

"That's nice," he said.

She could see the pitying look on his face, but he didn't say press her further. They listened to more hollering and clanking as the maintenance people worked.

"Would you want to have dinner with us sometime?" he asked.

"Because you feel sorry for me?"

"No, no, of course not. I think you're interesting," he said.

"For an old lady," she spit back.

"You're so prickly. Do you *want* to be alone?" he asked.

"Of course not. I'm alone because I suffered two miscarriages and my husband dropped dead during his prime from a genetic heart condition we never knew about. I am not alone because of my *personality* you little shit."

"Oh."

Micah sat there with his mouth hanging slightly open and his eyes wide before a thump and a whirring noise sounded. The elevator began to move down.

"Look, I'm sorry." He took deep breaths between the words, his condition deteriorating, but he pushed forward, explaining himself. "I didn't mean that. I just miss my family sometimes and I thought, I don't know, that maybe you did too."

Nat didn't respond. It was hard to miss what you never had. Or at least that's what she'd thought before, and then Robert had died, and the agony had increased tenfold. She couldn't get enough air in her lungs sometimes when she thought about all that she'd lost over the years.

Moments later the doors opened to freedom. Several maintenance men and a few EMTs stood at the ready. A man she assumed to be Ryan, Micah's boyfriend, was hovering behind the medical staff with two juice boxes, several protein bars, and a sweater. A female EMT ushered Micah out quickly while two male EMTs came in with a stretcher.

"Don't you dare," she pointed her finger at him. "Help me up and I'll be fine," she said.

The EMT with the 'semper fi' tattoo on his forearm and a buzzed head handed the stretcher to his co-worker.

"Yes ma'am," he said, before stretching out both hands for her to grip. He pulled her up like she weighed nothing and escorted her out.

"Thank you," she said, walking out of the elevator with her head held high.

Micah had shoved the sweatshirt on and was chugging his second juice box while the scrawny boyfriend with curly hair and dark thick-rimmed glasses fussed over him. An EMT fiddled with what she assumed was a glucose monitor as Micah sat in a chair.

"Ma'am, I need to get your vitals," the other EMT said. Nat let out a long breath.

"Fine, but I'll have you know this is a waste of time."

"I'm sure you're right, but this will help me sleep at night."

"She's pretty tough," Micah said when Nat sat down next to him in a makeshift area the EMTs had prepped for them. "You don't have to worry about her."

"If it's all the same," came the dry response. She gave them both a stern look but complied.

"Ryan, this is Natalya. Natalya, this is Ryan," Micah said.

Natalya reached her free hand out to shake Ryan's. He gave her a firm but gentle grasp before turning back to the EMT to pepper the short, blonde woman with details over Micah's health.

Mister military checked Nat's vitals and listened to her heart before he came to the obvious conclusion that Nat didn't need any medical attention.

"You're free to go," he said.

"As I thought," she said.

"The other elevators are working," one of the technicians said, overhearing she was done. "If you're not scarred from the last two hours of being stuck in there, you're welcome to use it to get home."

"Hasn't killed me yet, I guess," she said, getting up. "Good luck, kid," she said to Micah.

He already looked a million times better. The EMT had set up an

IV for him and his color was returning. Ryan and Micah said goodbye and Nat went to the working elevator bay where the maintenance man had been holding it open for her. She scanned her fob and pressed the button for twenty-two.

As the door began to close, a large foot stuck itself between them and they reopened. Micah ducked his head inside, IV bag and all. She heard Ryan yelling at him to sit back down.

"Friday at six. It's just dinner and you can leave if you hate it. Please," he said.

Those big brown eyes pleaded with her. Nat's stubborn old heart pretended not to want to go before the vision of sitting in her apartment by herself for another night jumped into her brain.

"Fine," she said, acting annoyed about it. Micah grinned.

"I swear you won't regret it," he said, backing up and allowing the doors to close again. "We'll see you soon Natalya."

"Call me Nat," she said. "All my friends do..." she trailed off.

The doors slammed shut but she heard his response anyway.

"Friday, Nat. Don't be late!"

sincerely yours

Izzy Thorpe

Do you remember that time we took that old refrigerator box and transformed it into a different world? We set it on the ground in your backyard and crawled inside, isolating ourselves away from the cloudy sky and vibrant, green grass. There was just enough room for us both to fit, squished in side by side. We brought markers and flashlights and became cave dwellers and homeowners and a tribe of two marking down our stories on the walls so that we could be remembered. We mapped out a future of dreams on cardboard that day. How young we must have felt to marvel at the permanence of a new home that could wash away in the rain.

Do you remember when we tried to figure out if cats really did always land on their feet? I don't think many other cats would be as forgiving as yours was. Like when we put him on a trampoline and bounced around? Or when we checked to see how fast a guinea pig could run in the tall grass, especially when motivated by vegetable treats? Or the difference it made when being playfully chased by either a doberman or a dachshund, as our collective feet pressed pathways through the grass? Do you remember how we mourned the end of your doberman's long, full life? Do you remember when your brother caught that black widow and made your family keep it as a pet? Until it laid eggs and you guys flushed the whole adventure down the toilet? Do you remember the way the bees floated by on the lazy summer afternoons? Or how the sunflowers peeked over the fence to watch us play in the warm sun?

Do you remember how loud it got when people would come over? The backyard would be filled with chattering voices; there was yelling and laughter. Do you remember when we each found someone to be our first love? It almost broke us at times. You were hurting, and you took some of that hurt out on me and I swear I almost walked out that day and never came back. I did come back, though. I never really left. We always had each other to talk to about boys, or whatever drama resulted as the product of youth. Do you remember when we sat in the shade of the creeping vines and agreed, in not so many words, that both of us were still too young to really know what love is?

Do you remember lounging blissfully in that white hammock? It was like a net, or a dream-catcher of sorts, collecting piles of memories. Do you remember how often that hammock flipped over and so unceremoniously tossed us to the ground? My favorite time, I think, is the evening of the first day of high school. We sat and shared stories, realizing that we were different, and that life was trying to lead us in different directions, but that some things never changed. Do you remember how we sat in the spring-cool mornings, waiting for the bus to come take us to school? We were too worldwise, by that point, to be making promises of forever to each other. But still we sat together and waited.

I know that so much time has passed, but every now and then I think about that cardboard box and the promises we made inside.

Sometimes, I want to tell you that I miss you. But sometimes I think that too much time has passed.

I do, though.
Miss you.

Sincerely yours,

walking the tracks

Amanda Kennedy

I slid open the glass door to the porch, stepped out, and hesitated. At eleven in the morning, it was already hot. I let my gaze rest on the pile of black garbage bags waiting for the next trip to the dump and weighed my options. Had I not been in active avoidance of my mom, I would've gone back inside to change into shorts. She and Jim were still asleep, and there was a good chance I could slip into my room without waking them. However, if I did wake them and Mom asked what I was doing, I would risk being marched into the kitchen to help her start lunch and resume our fight from last night. Besides, Jackie and I agreed we would both leave at exactly 11 o'clock. I closed the door softly behind me and cut across the yard to the train tracks.

Jim's massive workshop stood between his house and the tracks, and an assortment of vehicles in various states of disassembly were parked out front on the gravel driveway. A German Shepherd lifted his head from the shade of a rusty RV when I walked by but didn't bother getting up.

Following the train tracks in one direction led to wheat fields and cattle farms, while going in the opposite direction went into town, where I was headed. "Into town" was what people from out of town would say when they were driving in to pick up milk or cigarettes or meeting someone for a drink. The tracks cut straight through the middle of our small town, running right by the house Jackie shared with her dad, new stepmom, two siblings and three step-siblings. 'Step things', as she called them. By pickup truck, it wasn't more than a ten-minute drive down gravel roads, but on foot it would take me over an hour. This was the path to my best friend.

Jackie and I had been best friends since the eighth grade when she arrived at school mid-way through the year and had to sit out in gym class because she hadn't brought the required shorts and t-shirt. I regularly found ways to sit on the sidelines due to my strong dislike of both the teacher and the class. Competitive sports and strenuous exercise required amounts of enthusiasm and energy I did not possess. I varied my excuses; one day telling the teacher I had cramps, and the next day claiming to have forgotten my gym clothes. I was having a fake period the day the teacher sat Jackie next to me on the aluminum bleachers.

After the customary sharing of names and classes, and confirmation of a mutual loathing for physical exercise, we bonded over our dysfunctional families, our crazy mothers and our love of grunge rock music. By the end of the floor hockey game, we had logged a detailed catalog of each other's CD's, exchanged phone numbers, and made plans to eat lunch together.

By the end of the school year, people rarely saw one of us without the other.

I waded through the tall grass on the steep incline to the tracks, leaning forward until I reached them. The summer sun reflected off the rails and rocks. Droplets of oil oozed from the pores of the treated wooden ties like the sweat already forming on my belly. I pulled my baggy t-shirt up, tucked it under my bra and started walking.

Every time I made this trip, I tried out different strategies for walking the tracks. My first choice was always to try walking the rails, stepping one Converse shoe in front of the other, my skinny arms held out for balance. I would lose my balance again and again, until I eventually gave up and walked between the rails. From there, I would try to make my stride match the distance of the railway ties. The wide, wood planks were preferable to walking on the soft, loose gravel between them, but it was a frustrating exercise since the ties were too close together to accommodate an easy gait, yet too far apart for me to step to every other one. I would alternate between short baby steps and great clumsy strides, but wind up doing my best to walk as naturally as I could and putting up with the inconsistent and uneven ground.

The sun beat down from a cloudless sky and warmed the straight part at the top of my head. When I wasn't looking down, calculating my steps, I looked out at the fields of wheat on either side of the tracks. The landscape was dotted with small stands of trees clustered here and there, and I could see the horizon in every direction. I was alone, yet I didn't feel lonely in the same way I did in my bedroom, listening to my mom and Jim's murmured voices mixed with the sounds of the tv in the living room. Sitting behind my closed bedroom door, listening to Nirvana and looking at magazines, my loneliness felt as big as these wide-open skies. Before Jackie, I belonged to song lyrics, magazine models, and my dysfunctional family. After Jackie I belonged to inside jokes, swapping clothes, and the notes we passed between classes.

A light breeze slipped through my ripped-on-purpose jeans and fanned the sweat on my stomach. I ran my fingers through my hair, freeing it from my damp neck and strained my eyes to look down the track. If Jackie left when she said she would, I wouldn't be alone much longer. We always met halfway and continued into town together.

Seeing no sign of life down the track, I started humming a Nirvana song and humming turned to singing. I knew the words to every Nirvana song ever written and belted out the lyrics to Penny-royal Tea at a volume that would rival Kurt Cobain live in concert. My voice lifted and lifted, traveling further and further until I heard an echo return to me. I stopped singing and cast my eyes down the track to a wavering figure in the distance. Jackie looked like a mirage distorted by the heat rising off the tracks. I thought I could see her waving and I threw my hand in the air in return, knowing I was just as blurry to her as she was to me.

After a few more minutes of walking, I could make out more of her details and waved again at an almost mirror image of myself. Ripped jeans, long brown hair, skinny arms. I laughed when I saw her baggy shirt tucked up into her bra, too. We started walking faster, closing the gap, and yelled, "Hey" to each other when we got within shouting distance. A smile identical to my own was reflected back to me, and we embraced when we met.

Jackie launched into complaining about her 'step things', and we each stepped up onto a parallel rail, then reached across to hold hands, our arms spanning the width of the tracks. I told her about the fight with my mom and my steps landed sure and straight.

all the demons here in hell

Izzy Thorpe

It wasn't the violence that made Helen change. It wasn't the way her husband yelled at her nearly every night or the way he threw dishes on the ground in a rage when she asked for help, making her flinch and cower. It wasn't even the way he sat on the couch drinking beer and scratching his balls, demanding to know when dinner would be served.

It was the way he ignored her. He made her feel small and pretended that she didn't exist when he was annoyed. He filled her with a sense of rage and shame so great that she couldn't bury it deep down. So her eyes turned black and her skin grew rough and gray. Wings sprouted from her back and horns grew from her head. She changed until her husband had no choice but to pay attention to her. And this time, it was his turn to be afraid.

In the months after Helen's change, it felt like everything that could possibly go wrong was going wrong. Things had been difficult before, but now they felt impossible. With her husband gone, all of the household chores became her responsibility, not just the majority of them. Little things like dripping sinks and wobbly cabinet doors remained unfixed and the lawn soon became overgrown.

And while Helen could manage a household, society hadn't provided her the knowledge on how to fix a dishwasher nor did she have the funds to replace it. It took the pliers breaking in her claws with dishwasher parts scattered across the tile floor for Helen to decide that she would just be hand-washing everything from then on.

As much as she wanted to pretend things were the same with her family, they weren't. Her children didn't want to play with her as much, and while she kept telling herself that that's what happened when kids get older, part of her couldn't help but think it was because she was so different now. Helen's transformation didn't only change her outsides, she was different on the inside too. She was less vibrant than before and it was harder to fake being happy. Or maybe she had always been like this, and now other people could see it.

Her children kept asking her, "what happened to Daddy?" and even though as a mom she was supposed to have all of the answers, she didn't know what to say. She changed the subject and continued to ferry them to school and extracurriculars.

Things weren't much better at work. Helen could have sworn that she was next in line for a promotion, but she was passed over.

"Is it because of the horns?" she had asked her manager.

"It's not *not* because of the horns," he told her. Which everyone knew meant it was definitely because of the horns.

Officially, they told her it was because her personality was too "abrasive" for client relations even though she was juggling the most clients. She even handled the more difficult clients, the ones that asked for too many things on top of requesting everything be done twice. She did it without complaint.

Everyone knew that Helen was the one who deserved that promotion. Nothing was said aside from the hushed whispers of office gossip which followed her around. Helen was managing a major account and all anyone wanted to talk about was how she looked – that and what happened to her husband.

Everywhere she went, Helen felt like people were staring at her. She had lived in the same small town all of her life, so while she didn't know everyone, there was still a sense of familiarity. It got especially bad in the places where she did know people. At her son's soccer practice she could hear the other moms whispering, acting like they knew exactly what had gone down between her and her ex-husband.

"I heard she ate him!" One of the moms whispered, sending the other moms into a fit of giggles.

"I heard she put him away in the attic so she can take him out at Halloween and scare all the children." More giggles.

"What are you talking about? All she has to do is stand outside on Halloween and that'll scare the kids shitless." The giggles devolved into raucous laughter and all Helen could do was pretend that she couldn't hear them. For once, Helen was grateful for her new gray skin because it covered up the creeping flush on her face. She held her head low until it was time to leave.

"Careful, or you'll end up like her!" More laughter.

She was much larger now, but had never felt quite this small.

It was the sign outside of the bar that Helen couldn't get out of her head. She had passed the dingy little place on her way home last week. The outside was covered in wooden slats and the bar's name, Hell, was hand painted and hung on chains above the door.

However, it was the folding sign set up on the sidewalk that drew Helen's attention. It read: 'Abandon All Hope, Ye Who Enter Here: Free shots for anyone having a rough time'. In even smaller letters below, the sign read: 'One Shot Per Personal Tragedy'.

When work was finally over on Friday, Helen dropped her kids off with her mother and went to Hell. She put on her best outfit, or at least her best outfit that could still fit over the wings. She had attempted makeup, but all her beige foundations looked off on her gray skin. Everything pooled in her skin's rough, stone-like texture, making any makeup attempt fruitless.

At last she smeared a bit of black eye shadow around her eyes, but ultimately washed it off because she thought it made her look too slutty and was not something a woman of her age should be wearing. She didn't want to make it look like she was asking for attention. Not when she already looked the way that she did.

Helen entered the bar with scrunched shoulders and a purse clutched tightly in her claws. The entrance led to a set of dimly-lit stone stairs. She followed them down to a larger opening with stone walls, wooden tables and chairs, all poorly illuminated by a series of ill-conceived neon lights.

It was darker than she was expecting, even though the bar was named Hell. In the middle of the space there was a large stone bar top that looked carved out from the floor. Helen went straight to the bar and ordered a shot to start. The bartender didn't even question her about her personal tragedy, just set out 3 shot glasses in a row and filled them to the top with vodka. Before she could say thanks, the bartender had already moved on to serving someone else. She quickly downed the first shot and erupted into a fit of coughing.

"Hey." There was a drunk man next to her that she hadn't noticed at first. She tried her best to ignore him. "Hey," he said again, until at last Helen hesitantly looked over at him. His face was ruddy and he swayed in his seat like he was on a boat in the middle of the sea. Helen looked away again, too afraid of accidentally initiating a conversation.

"HEY!" the drunk man shouted, "I'm talking to you!"

"Yes?" Helen looked over again, head bowed in submission.

"You know, let me get a few more drinks in me, and I'd be willing to sit on a face like yours. I bet you like it nasty." He smiled dreamily like he was proud of himself, as if he would be doing her a favor. Inside her chest, Helen's heart sank.

"What about my face?" A woman came up from behind Helen, making her jump and turn. Helen was shocked by how much this woman looked like her. They had the same rough, textured skin, the same horns, and the same large wings. The biggest difference was that this woman had much longer teeth, so long that they stuck out past her lips, even with her mouth closed. That, and her eyes were a lovely shade of red whereas Helen's were a deep black.

The man scowled at this new woman, taking her in.

"Although, I have to warn you, I'm a little peckish. I might just bite it off." She punctuated her statement by snapping her jaw and biting the air. Her long teeth only added to the effect. Helen had never been great at reading people, but in this moment, she could see the man imagining what it would feel like if this woman actually 'bit it off'. He glared at them both and walked away mumbling to himself. Helen could barely make out the words "stupid bitches" as he left.

"Thanks," Helen said as the woman took the stool next to her and held up a finger to the bartender. "But what if he does something like wait outside the bar for us to come out?"

The woman turned to Helen with a look of utter confusion. "So?"

Helen blinked. "He could hurt us?"

The woman laughed. "I could rip the flesh from his bones with my teeth."

Helen took the second shot and scrunched her face at the bitter taste. "You never know," she mumbled into the empty glass.

"I'm Margaret, but you can call me Maggie," the woman said, holding out her hand for Helen to shake. Hesitating, Helen reached out and gripped Maggie's hand in her own.

"Helen."

She could feel the gentlest sensation of claws against her rough skin.

"So what brings you here, Helen? I haven't seen you in Hell before." Maggie asked as the bartender placed a whiskey sour in front of her without needing to confirm her order.

"It was the sign."

"Free shots?"

Helen shook her head.

"No, the 'Abandon All Hope, Ye Who Enter Here'. I've been feeling pretty dang hopeless lately, so I thought, why not?"

Maggie nodded as if this made complete sense. "I hate to pry, but is it because…" she gestured to all of Helen with her chin.

"It's not not because I'm like this." In her head she heard her manager using the same double negative to try and soften the blow from what he really wanted to say. "Okay, yeah, it is because of…" Helen admitted, but instead of finishing her sentence she simply gestured to her body.

"Want to talk about it?" Maggie took a sip of her drink.

"What about you?" Helen bristled, adjusting her wings. "Do you want to talk about it?" She hadn't meant to sound rude, but still hoped it was enough to change the topic of conversation.

Maggie shrugged, "I was attacked."

Helen sat up straight and turned to look at Maggie, surprised.

"He came out of nowhere," Maggie continued, "it was dark and late and of course there was no one around. But I'm sure he knew that. He shoved me to the ground and tried to hold me down, although I was bucking and kicking like a wild horse. I could feel him trying to rip my clothes off, grabbing at me, and all I could think over and over was 'not like this'. The next thing I felt was my body changing. I barely processed what was different before I was fighting back hard. It's true that I'm a biter." Maggie chuckled, but the laugh was dry and humorless.

There was a pause between them.

"Then what?" Helen asked.

Maggie reached for her drink and downed the rest of it. She swallowed hard and held up a finger to order another one. Helen took the third shot, and placed the empty glass in line with the others. Already, her head was swimming.

"I don't know. I left. I don't know if he was alive or dead when I left, I didn't check. I don't think I hurt him bad enough for it to be too serious, I was only trying to get free. But the way my teeth and claws are... I don't know."

"Oh," Helen said and it didn't feel like enough, but it was all she could think to say.

"Yeah," Maggie replied and both women sat in silence for a minute fiddling with their empty glasses. Around them, the chatter of the other patrons filled the air. Someone laughed hard in the background, the sound echoing in the cavernous space.

"I think I have to leave now," Helen announced unceremoniously, grabbing her bag. She stood up and faced the door before turning back once more towards Maggie. "Lovely to meet you, but you know, I need to pick up the kids."

"Sure," Maggie smiled, ignoring the impromptu excuse.

Helen set some bills on the table, enough to cover both their drinks despite the shots being free plus a tip, then bolted towards the stairs and didn't look back.

Helen spent the next week thinking about Maggie and what

happened to her. Her mind went in circles trying to figure out what it was about Maggie's story that made her so uncomfortable that she would rather flee than confront it. It made her question herself and her own transformation as well. Was she embarrassed of what had happened to her? Did she think Maggie should have been embarrassed as well?

At work, Helen was distracted by what happened in Hell. The whispers still trailed after her in the office, the rumor mill constantly churning out new theories. Helen noticed the words didn't hurt her the same way they did before. She was too busy feeling a confusing swirl of emotions, rather than worrying about what she should be feeling. She was almost too distracted to notice her manager berating the man who got the promotion over her for mismanaging his client. Almost.

When Friday came, Helen followed the same routine as the week before. She dropped the kids off with her mom, then spent far too long getting ready. Again, Helen questioned every possible choice of attire. What this dress would make people think of her, or if those shoes would make her look too tall. She did apply a little bit of dark eye-shadow and almost wiped it off before thinking of Maggie. Maggie would leave the eye-shadow on.

Helen made it to Hell, walked down the stone staircase, and entered the bar. There were fewer people than the previous week, but there were still enough people for unintelligible conversations to fill any silence with white noise. She looked around for any sign of Maggie, then at last, without seeing her, sat in the same spot as before. After racking her brain for the name of any drink, she ordered a Long Island Iced Tea because she preferred the taste of tea to more bitter drinks like whiskey or bourbon.

"You're back. I thought I scared you away for good."

Helen whipped around at the sound of the familiar voice. Maggie took the seat next to her, the same spot as before.

"I thought... yeah. I'm here" Helen managed, making Maggie smile. Maggie ordered a whiskey sour and Helen took the chance to take a big gulp of her drink. It did not taste very much like tea.

"Look, I'm sorry. I didn't mean to pressure you," Maggie started, "I didn't tell you what happened to me to try and make you share your story or anything. I just... I just wanted to. I thought you would understand."

Helen took another large sip of her drink until the fuzziness filled her head. The bartender placed Maggie's drink in front of her and she took a sip, waiting for Helen to be ready to speak. At last she said, "for me it was nothing like that. It was nothing dramatic or anything. I just... I saw the dishes in the sink. They weren't even dirty. I had asked my husband, my ex-husband, to put them away.

"I know it doesn't sound like a lot, but I had been asking for days and I came home to a pile of dishes sitting on the counter, dishes that I had washed you know? I had done all of the hard work and all he had to do was put them away. And it had been a stinker of a day too. I had been asking for days and he couldn't do this one simple thing? I snapped."

Maggie nodded in understanding. "So you ate him."

It could have been the absurdity of the situation or the liquor from Helen's "tea", but she burst into laughter.

"No, I asked for a divorce."

"Next best thing."

"You should have seen his face," Helen was still laughing, "he just about shit his pants when he saw me looking like this."

Maggie smiled, "I wish I could have. I'm sure it was something."

Helen sighed, "almost makes it worth it, becoming a monster."

The smile faded from Maggie's face.

"You're not."

"Not what?"

"A monster. You're not a monster."

Helen blinked, unsure of how to respond, "But I have horns."

Maggie snorted, "Didn't know that was the criteria."

"People shouldn't have horns."

"Says who?"

Helen blanked at Maggie's question.

"Have you ever done anything bad with your horns? hurt someone?"

"No, but—" Helen started.

"Are you a worse person for having horns?"

"I don't know, but—"

"But what?"

"They make me ugly. Look at my skin, my wings, my eyes are all black for pete's sake."

Maggie stopped for a moment and looked at Helen, really looked.

"You know, I thought this when I first saw you, but I really think we look alike. There are some differences, sure, but overall, we look pretty similar. Do you think I'm ugly?"

Helen almost said "no," but before the word could escape from her lips, she stopped herself. She thought about it, really thought. She felt the same way as Maggie, when she first saw her all she could think about was how similar they looked. She thought about Maggie's rough skin, her horns and her wings. At last she decided that no, she never looked at Maggie like she was ugly. In fact, she thought there was something admirable about her. Beautiful, even.

"No," Helen said.

"If I'm not ugly, how can you be?" The silence hung between

them once more until Maggie spoke again.

"I told you what happened with… that guy. I didn't even check, I just left. Does that make me a monster?"

It was the guilt, Helen realized. She was so drawn to Maggie because she could recognize the guilt that she was feeling in herself. Someone else did something bad and they were monsters because of it. Except that they weren't, not really. But that didn't make the guilt go away.

"I think it makes you human."

Maggie nodded and waited for Helen to continue.

"I get it, okay? I do. I know we didn't *do anything*. All you did was fight to survive and all I did was ask for some stupid divorce. We wanted to be free and we became monsters because of it. And I know. I know we're not really monsters, we're the way we are despite the horns and the wings. But how come that doesn't stop the stares? How come I'm still treated like a criminal, an outsider? I'm somehow completely unapproachable and still some sort of hussy. That doesn't even make sense. It's not the horns that make me a monster, it's the way people look at them." Helen tried to stop the words from coming, but her head was swimming from her earlier drink and she couldn't stop her volume from rising.

Maggie raised her glass, took a small sip, then placed it gently back on the bartop.

"You say you can't just ignore the stares and the gossip, but what are your other options? What are you going to do about it?"

Turning away, Helen muttered, "I don't know."

"Are you going to say something to stop them?"

Helen pouted. "I could. If I wanted to."

"Then do it. Or don't. You can stand up for yourself if you want to or you can ignore all of the gossipy bullshit that is bothering you so much. I don't care, hun, but clearly you do. So do something about it instead of wallowing in self pity."

"I'm sorry for getting loud," Helen started. "You're right." The weight of her outburst was hitting her. The momentum had gone and the all too familiar shame and sting of her own insecurity had arrived.

"Girl, it's okay to get loud sometimes. That's kinda the point I'm trying to make."

Helen thought for a minute then sighed, "Okay. I'll try. Your advice is pretty good. I don't know if it'll be that easy to ignore everyone else or even stand up for myself, but I can try."

"Good." Maggie nodded. "And don't forget you can be loud about it."

"I'm perfect just the way I am!" Helen announced in her loudest indoor voice just as the bartender stepped up to them to check on their drinks.

"Preach," the bartender said in the uninterested tone of a man swamped with work, wiping the bartop in front of them. "So do you ladies want another round?"

They both stared at him wide-eyed then nodded, but when he tried to take Helen's cup, Maggie stopped him.

"Let's try something sweet and fruity for her instead, hun."

"Sure, coming right up," The bartender took the glasses away and started mixing the drinks. As soon as he was out of earshot, they both erupted into giggles.

"I guess I'm what you'd call a bit of an obnoxious drunk," Helen commented, burying her face in her hands while watching the bartender from the crack in her fingers.

Chuckling, Maggie called out to him, "go easy on the liquor for hers, will you?" Without looking up he flashes the ladies a thumbs up, earning more giggles from them. She sighed then turned back to Helen.

"It's never easy when the world sees you in a different way than you see yourself. It can feel like maybe they're all right and you're the thing that needs changing."

Helen reached for her drink to fiddle with before remembering the bartender had already taken it away.

"Can I ask you something?" Maggie said.

"At this point you can ask me just about anything."

"Would you do anything different? If you could go back to how you were before, would you still ask for a divorce even knowing what would happen to you?"

Helen swallowed hard and thought about what her life was like with her ex-husband. Then she thought harder about what her life was like now.

"Yes, I think I would."

"It's the same for me. I was always going to fight back, no matter what it took. The world could judge me or I could judge myself, I could feel all the misplaced guilt and shame, but I was always going to fight back." Maggie tapped on the bartop with both hands waiting for their drinks to arrive. "It took me a long time to forgive myself and a longer time to realize that I didn't need forgiving. I've spent years practicing what it was like to not look at myself like I was a monster."

"Years, huh?"

The bartender returned with the whiskey sour and something pink with fruit on a stick and an umbrella.

Helen tried it and her eyes went wide.

"It's really good! It tastes like lemonade!"

Maggie chuckled. "Good. Stop drinking all of the drinks you don't like the taste of."

They both took welcome sips of their drinks. It was the first drink here that didn't make Helen cough or wince from the taste.

"If," Helen began, "I were to stop by next week, do you think you could help me pick another drink that I would like?"

"I suppose so. If you want." Maggie grinned at the invitation.

Helen held up her glass for a toast. "This is how you do it, right? It's how they do it in the movies."

Both women erupted into a fit of giggles.

"You don't have to change for anyone," Maggie said, "the world can't make you a monster. I'll be here until you can remember that on your own."

Maggie raised her glass too, "to learning to love your new look."

Helen smiled at the warmth she felt from someone who was a complete stranger not too long ago. A soft clink sounded as Maggie's glass reached Helen's.

"To finding someone who sees the real you."

family

palm to palm

Allison Matalone

She doesn't remember when it started, it was after the divorce, after her mom had moved to another state with her little sister. Since she had been finishing up high school, it hadn't made sense to start over mid senior year. She had shared a room with her sister for as long as she could remember.

Whenever her sister had cried in the night, she climbed into her bed and curled around her, and they would fall asleep hands clasped.

One night when it was a little too dark and she was a little too lonely and the cicadas were too loud outside her window she rolled onto her side and laced her own hands together and was finally able to fall asleep.

As the years passed it went from infrequent to monthly, weekly, and then nightly.

At 22, lying next to her first serious boyfriend after her first time, she, after much debating, placed her hand in his open palm. He rolled away. That relationship lasted eight more days. With her next three boyfriends one had sweaty palms, one slept fists clenched like he did 12 rounds each night and the third would wake at the slightest touch.

Then she met her husband. Whose hand was always open and when she brushed her hand against his he would clasp hers and the slight pressure would lull her to sleep. She knew every whorl, every crease, every detail down to the slight bend in one finger from catching a fastball with the wrong hand. And on the nights he wasn't beside her, she would only have to close her eyes and picture his hand and she could sleep.

When their baby came sometimes he would sleep between them.

That first night, her husband rolled to his side and placed his open palm between their pillows above the baby's head, his lips quirked, and with her face hidden in her pillow she took his hand.

And then one day he wasn't there any more. When she closes her eyes all she sees is his hand after the accident in the hospital, bandaged and broken. She lies awake at night, her hand in the divot where he used to sleep. She stares for hours at the far wall until exhaustion forces her to sleep. She tries holding her own hand, but her hand is too cold and too small, there is no comforting bend to brush a finger over, or a rough callous to stroke.

One night their son wakes with a cry. She rushes to his room and cuddles him close. He is almost too big to be carried, but she does so settling him on her side. He's wrapped around her crying softly and she strokes his back. When the sobs have abated and his limbs have loosened their hold, they lay curled towards each other, he takes his small smooth hand and places it in hers. She smiles and the dark hides her glistening eyes. At last mother and son fall asleep.

sigh

Christine Urgello

Sigh...
I can only do so much
to keep you by my side:
cuddle, giggle, sing a lullaby;
and you will only stay so long
before Spotifying something
a bit more interesting
than my song.
Ah, but,
if I could,
I would weld you to my hip;
or, to be less extreme, perhaps
just bind you to my side with duct tape...
Would that you would
stay a little bit longer
in the circle of my arms
where I can shield you
from the flack and flurry
of a madly spinning world;
where your tiny hands can hold me
and keep me whole; where I can feel you
and remember who I am;
where the scent of you
brings me home.

bindings of blood

Rose Pulford

The bindings of blood
Carry the weight of generations
Pass down memories and trauma
Through the waves of time

THE PROPHECY

lee graham

the girl with
coiled crown
kneels before
his gilded tongue

lips parted
beneath the
pyrite fountain
reckoning

glittering truth
and praying
something bright
slips inside

her plastic heart
from before
their blood recalled
that old

pulsing sump
desperate to
mistake anything
gold

for honey and
sticky eternity

a sister's love

Tara Henderson

Content Warning: contains depictions of physical abuse and alludes to sexual abuse.

Chelsea shoved her hands underneath her thighs, enveloped in smooth, white tights, covered by a ruffled, cotton slip and a pale, pink dress with tiny, blue flowers. This trick, the capture of her hands, was how I taught her to keep the wiggles at bay. If she wasn't reverent, our father would notice, even from eight pews ahead, sitting next to the Bishop. Both men stared into the crowd, eyes humble and mouths set straight. If our father didn't notice, surely one of our *dear sweet* brothers would tell on her for the pleasure of watching one of their sisters be disciplined.

At fifteen, I was already well-versed in the role I played. As the oldest girl, I was Mother's right-hand. Whether it be in the kitchen or at church, I was to help whenever there was a need. I faux-smiled at my dad and swallowed my disgust at the hypocrisy of it all.

Chelsea looked to her left, where I sat, with our two older brothers. Our parents insisted that we were always in age order: Matthew, myself (Madeleine), and Mark. Chelsea sat exactly in the middle of the flock. To her right sat our little sister, Mary, then Mother, and last was baby Luke (not such a baby at six-years old). The young ones had to be separated by Mother to avoid disrupting the congregation. The Oates Family had three girls and three boys – the Lord had *blessed* us with perfect symmetry, in the same manner He had designed rose petals, corn husks and butterflies.

"And because of the Savior's atonement, we can purify our hearts to become more like him, loving others as He would." Our father had started his talk while Chelsea was looking back and forth at us. Father had been assigned to give a talk today on loving others. Hypocrisy personified. Chelsea and I had overheard him complaining to Mother last night about having to give a talk when he was already signed up to teach the lesson in Sunday School. At our church it was well-understood that saying no was unacceptable. Not when you were in the service of the Lord.

Mark, who was thirteen and only fourteen months older than her, elbowed Chelsea in the side. She didn't flinch, being used to the sharp pains inflicted by our brothers for their amusement. She simply shook her head and stared straight ahead. He pinched the flesh on the back of her arm. I didn't do anything because there was nothing to do; if I intervened, he would inflict worse harm later. My insides boiled over with helplessness.

Father looked down to read from his outline, and the little ones were occupying Mother's attention, so Chelsea snatched the note Mark was holding for her, and he finally let go of her skin.

Setting aside the charade of reverence, Chelsea ignored my training and opened the note. She let out a snort of stifled laughter when she saw the sketch Mark had made of Father. Oversized nose, three comb-over wisps for hair, and red eyes. Mark did have a knack for funny drawings; he wasn't all bad.

Father sat down after bearing testimony of Christ and the Bishop announced that the Sacrament would be blessed and passed around. "Oh God, the Eternal Father, we ask thee in the name of thy Son, Jesus Christ..." The cadence of the familiar prayer marched me through an accounting of my actions of the week. Had I been holy? I was sure I had: helping mom when she asked, cleaning my room without being told, perfect scores at school, nice to my friends, memorized three scriptures, and even helped the neighbor who was cursed with rheumatoid arthritis (due to her sinful childhood, according to Father). I breathed a sigh of relief. I had nothing to ask forgiveness for today.

The next three and a half hours of church continued like every other Sunday, complete with potluck lunch provided by the women. When lunch was over, the kids ran amuck in the grassy area just outside the chapel doors, while I pushed my resentment aside and cleaned up the meal with the other teenage girls. When the work was done, I went outside and called the kids over. We gathered around the full-sized maroon van waiting for our parents.

When a click unlocked the door, Matthew slid it open and scrambled to get inside. Maroon carpet, curtains, and seats greeted us. Matthew and Mark pushed their way in to claim the captain's chairs, Matthew flipping up the skirt of Chelsea's dress as she passed. I gave him a look and he made space for the rest of us to pass. Even though I'm taller than both brothers, as a girl I'm accustomed to acquiescing to their whims. The four of us had to squeeze onto the back row bench seat. Mary and Luke sat in the middle and I buckled the single lap belt over both of them. It would take the entire ride home for the air conditioning to reach the back of the van. There was no relief from the oppressive air: not here, not at home, not ever.

"Quiet down back there," Father yelled while climbing into the van. He preferred us to be silent. He started the engine and turned up his favorite instrumental hymns CD on the stereo.

Sunday afternoons were filled with silent scripture study, piano practice, or prayer. Whoever Father caught fidgeting or playing with a smuggled toy was forced to skip dinner, or worse, had their name posted on the fridge to remind the entire family and any visitors of their transgression.

Chelsea sat on her hands again. Over the last few months her behaviors had taken on a compulsive nature: eyes darting to and fro, startling at sudden noises, and I had a front row seat to the light in her eyes diminishing. Her childhood zest was fading away with each passing day. At twelve years old she was becoming too aware of her place in my parents' world. Instead of futile anger, I was becoming more and more resolved to do something.

From way up in the driver's seat Father asked Mother, who was always in the co-pilot chair, never allowed to drive if he was in the car. "Mother – how long have you had that dress?"

Here we go again, I dug my fingernails into my folded arms to keep myself from saying anything.

Mother looked down at the navy blue dress with abstract white squiggles and shrugged, knowing there wasn't a correct answer. Too old and Father would accuse her of trying to look poor in front of the rest of the congregation. Too new and he would be upset at her for being wasteful of the family resources.

"I don't remember it." Father continued as he turned the van down our street. "Do you think it's appropriate for church? I mean, you look lovely, and if you think it's appropriate. But maybe, it's a bit too...provocative."

I shook my head, Chelsea watched me from her side of the bench seat. She was always watching me, taking cues from my behavior. The pressure not to react was building as my younger siblings got older. I knew how to keep myself safe, but who knew what her teenage years would be like. Would she, too, be capable of staying true to herself while also feigning devotion?

Chelsea peered her head around the captain's chairs to inspect Mother's dress. It was a button-up with collar, mid-calf, and loose fitting. Father thought it wasn't okay for church and I watched as

Chelsea looked down at her own dress to judge. Seated, her knees were visible, but the hem fell modestly to the knees when standing. She shifted on the bench, tugging her hemline lower. Mary, only six years old, did the same. I felt like vomiting.

At home, we filed out of the van: boys first, then the littles, followed by Chelsea and me who always took up the rear. Bellies full from the potluck and lips sealed out of fear, we filed into the house. Father headed straight to his office to study and Mother to the kitchen to prepare his afternoon tea. He was not to be disturbed under any circumstances. Everyone stayed in their church clothes. Chelsea and I followed Mother to the kitchen. The table needed to be set and everything plated for a five o'clock dinner. We would be serving the Bishop's family tonight – an honor indeed. *More like torture.*

I mirrored Mother's rhythm through the kitchen, going through the motions with the practiced ease of years of homemaking. Father had approved the menu a week ago when the invitation was extended, and by 4:55 dinner was warming in the oven, the table was set, and we all had our hands washed and hair brushed. The doorbell summoned Father from his office to greet the Bishop, his wife, and their four kids.

Dinner passed, not quickly enough, with compliments to the chefs, concern for the congregation, warnings about public school, and extended farewells until we would meet again at Wednesday's youth group. It was a normal occurrence, of course, to have families from church over for Sunday dinner but it never got easier pretending to be a happy family in our own home. It felt even more dishonest than when we did it elsewhere. My shoulders relaxed watching Father wave to the Bishop's family as they pulled away. The relief was premature, of course.

"To your rooms. Now," Father commanded. All six of us filed down the short hall to our respective bedrooms. We all knew better than to protest with a command like that.

The berating was heard by us all. *Mother must be desperate for attention. Doesn't Father provide her enough love and affection? Bishop's wife must have felt like Jezebel herself was serving them dinner. That dress*, he told her, *was provocative. Why hadn't she changed?* Mother's voice was quiet, not pleading. Father would not stand for piteous begging. Mother kept her voice humble and claimed innocence. Bishop's wife was Mother's best friend, and would never think of Mother behaving untoward.

Most people don't know that a fist is not noiseless and can be heard through the paper thin walls of a modest home, such as ours. Mother's soft voice soon turned to muffled sobs; her attempts at hiding the altercation from us was useless; I'm not sure how she thought we didn't know. Most of the time Mother's bruises were hidden but Chelsea had asked me about the flashes of blue and green she'd seen when Mother was changing or rolling up her sleeves to wash dishes. "Father," I would respond.

On Father's worst days his passion would even be turned towards Matthew. I could tell that Matthew, who was almost as big as Father, was nearing the end of his patience with the abuse. I prayed for the day when Matthew would strike him back.

I read stories to the little ones with hushed cheerful tones to distract them. Chelsea snuggled in between them as they gripped onto the hippo stuffed animals that Grandma had dropped off. We weren't allowed to speak to her, Father's orders, and he never allowed her into the house, but the stuffed animals were a treasured assurance that someone, somewhere cared, saw, knew.

I shared a room with Chelsea, Mary, and Luke, so when the sobbing ended and we heard the click of the deadbolt to Mother and Father's bedroom, I put my finger to my lips, not that they needed to be told to shush, and led them to the bathroom to get ready for bed. Soon we were all tucked in, and another Sunday was over. Monday would bring the safety of a school day for us children. It also meant that Mother would be safe from Father while he was away at work.

But Monday was tomorrow and not too long after we tucked ourselves in, the door creaked open and Matthew came in. He nudged Chelsea's shoulders to wake her. She feigned sleep, like she had the last two times he came, just as I had trained her to do. But this time he yanked her pillow out from under her head and she startled. I jumped down from the top bunk, stumbled across the tiny room, and pushed him towards the door, hissing at him that I would tell Father if he didn't leave Chelsea alone. I closed the door with a quiet click so the little ones wouldn't wake up and followed Matthew to his room.

After school the next day Chelsea and I sat together under the shade of an oak tree while waiting to walk the little ones home. Chelsea pulled a Coca-Cola out of her backpack and set it on the picnic table. I stared into the brick wall of the building as the sizzling Coke turned flat. Chelsea picked it up and offered it to me. My fake smile did nothing to reassure her and she set the drink back on the table.

"I'm going to talk to Mom today," I said, still spellbound by the brick wall.

"I can do it with you."

"No. She doesn't need to be mad at both of us," I said.

Chelsea rested her head on my shoulder and I kissed her forehead – our silent ritual of comfort, void of shame or expectations.

Mother was waiting for us in the kitchen with an afternoon snack of blueberry muffins and ice cold milk. Once we finished, I told Chelsea to take the littles to play games in our room. A look of concern crossed Chelsea's face, but I shook my head, determined to keep her free of any blame or trouble.

Once toys were set out and play was under way, I saw Chelsea peek out the door, down the short hallway, and into the kitchen, unnoticed by Mother. I may not be a woman yet, but at sixteen I knew what was right and what was wrong and I was determined to make Mother listen.

"Mother, I told you before, he –" I tried.

"I won't hear it." Mother interrupted, "Matthew is a good Christian boy. He just earned his Eagle Scout and he goes to church every week without whining."

I lowered my voice, not wanting Chelsea to hear all of it.

"You have to do something...Chelsea...the others..." I attempted to explain what was happening without being too explicit. She would shut down if I went too far.

"Do you want me to tell the Bishop about your sinful accusation?" Mother's voice quieted but the look of disbelief, even anger, remained. "My precious son is not at fault; Madeleine, you have always been jealous of him and these allegations are yet another attempt to make him look bad."

I pleaded, doing my best to appeal to Mother's maternal instincts, but her heart was as hardened as Father's.

After dinner I told Mother and Father that Chelsea and I would like to clean the kitchen as a gift to give Mother the night off. Such fine daughters, Father praised, and invited Mother to go for a walk. Once the front door shut, I grabbed the hiking daypacks from the basement. Wordless, we packed snacks and water, then moved to our bedrooms and shoved in as much clothing as would fit.

Mary and Luke were watching us. "Do you guys want to come?" I asked them. Their eyes lit up. "We won't see Mother or Father for a long time."

"They want to be with us. It's not safe to leave them." Chelsea added, knowing Matthew would come for them next. I had warned Chelsea to never be alone with him and even though Chelsea couldn't possibly understand what I had been going through for years, she trusted me. I didn't want her to know.

It was time to leave the present in the past. The future was unknown, but safety would never be found within these walls. Nothing came from pleading with Mother, so our only choice was to flee.

When the deadbolt clicked that night, not a single pair of eyes in our room were closed. We were ready.

Five miles was my estimate. It had been ten years since our family made the journey, but I recalled the way–I hoped. Dimly lit streets led us a mile down the country road and into town. Chelsea had the little ones take turns getting piggy-back rides. I was carrying too much as it was.

We passed the McDonald's whose bright lights tore through the night. The barber shop reminded me of our brothers–I looked away. Even though I knew this was their best chance at a good future, I was heartbroken to tear the littles from Mother and Father. We passed a nail salon, Pizza Hut, donut shop, and finally the corner store where we turned left.

We tried to stick to the shadows. The little ones' feet started to drag, their energy running low. Not a single car passed us as we snuck through our sleepy town.

Just after we turned was Father's office. Righteous Accounting: Taxes, Bookkeeping, and More. I paused, staring at the large glass window. Chelsea picked up a rock and hurled it. I smiled at her and did the same. Even the little ones joined in, hurling stones, and shattering the glass. A perfect reflection of our shattered lives.

We threw until we ran out of rocks and our arms ached.

I looked at my watch. "We better hurry. Grandma will be going to bed soon." Grandma was a night owl according to Mother, but owls need to sleep too.

At eleven fifty-three, after peering through the peephole and seeing four tired children, Grandma opened the door. *Her dears. Her sweet grandbabies had walked all the way in the middle of the night.* When Grandma opened her arms I fell into them and wept like a baby. Grandma was a stranger to Mary and Luke and only a faded memory to Chelsea. But if I trusted this gray-haired woman with kind eyes, then they would too.

We left behind the wasteland of our home to find a safe one. I had to be their savior because the one our parents believed in had never been there for us.

When Mother tried to take us home the next day, after figuring out where we were, we clung to Grandma. Mother called the police, arguing that she had a right to us, her children. But I had been documenting the abuse: dates, times, and on occasion, photos of Mother's bruises (without Mother knowing). A judge ruled that Grandma would have custody until the investigations were complete.

I sat in the courtroom for what felt like weeks. The investigation into Father's abusive behavior revealed that Father had stolen thousands of dollars worth of donations and gambled them away. Father denied everything and was only sentenced to five years in prison because Mother wouldn't take the stand to testify against him.

Matthew, on the other hand, was charged with abuse. I took the stand and spared no detail, even with my Mother's quiet sobs echoing throughout the courtroom. Once I came forward, word got around at church about my assault and two other teenage girls spoke up. With three voices accusing him of sexual assault, the judge sentenced him to twenty-five years.

The night after the last day in court, sipping chamomile tea in Grandma's kitchen, Chelsea leaned her head on my shoulder and the tension melted away. This time, rightly so.

entering re-life

Carisa H-K

A short story preview from the forthcoming novel,
FIGMENTS (THE RE-LIFE STORY: BOOK ONE).
©2024

Soft music plays in the kitchen. Muted and primal, its rhythm warms the body with heartbeat alignment. Next to a gray island countertop, a gentle curved figure hunches over a simmering pot. Her fingers are long and delicate along the spoon, as she swirls its contents. After taking a satisfactory whiff, she straightens her torso – revealing a sturdy and stable elegance. With legs in A-frame and shoulders squared and tall, she continues to stir. She appears poised, even in leggings, and even as her oversized gray sweatshirt drips from her shoulder. More than one spiteful brown curl escapes her headband.

Ellede loved making a special, fragrant dish each weekend. This time, a Ghanaian one-pot delicacy – a hearty and rich stew of chicken, peanut, and spicy peppers. This is enough for several heaping servings: their family meal for the day, plus a little extra for lunch tomorrow. Plantain chips sit ready in their bag to help scoop up the savory sauce.

Again inhaling the aroma, she is reminded of coconut korma... or is it Thai satay? She takes pride in crafting all kinds of global flavor – from jerk chicken to a rich homemade bolognese with pasta. Her kitchen is where the look of a matzo ball mirrors the rice balls sitting ready to swim in her Groundnut soup today. It's not all that different. Looks similar, even sometimes smells similar – and all tastes divine.

Home is quiet except for the sound of wind chimes now mingling with the ambient rhythms. Loved ones remain asleep in the next room, but she is buzzing. Thoughts swirl around her head about her new job, much like the stew swirling around the pot. She starts on Monday. While she is confident, she knows this is still a challenge unlike any she has faced before.

Can I handle it? Fake it 'till I make it, I guess. In the next instant she admonishes herself. *I'm prepared, and that will carry me through this new challenge. Just like it always has.* Her experience at a competing server company equipped her well. And her double major in Psychology and Communications plus subsequent MBA can't hurt either.

She leans down toward the pot again for a taste. Smacking the tip of her tongue to her plump lips, she looks skyward, pondering: *Something is missing.* Unable to reach a quick conclusion, she whirls around to face the island countertop opposite the stove. To the rest of the room, she queries: "Recipe please?"

Three other women, standing quiet moments before, step forward to surround her on the walls. On her left, two are present on a floor-to-ceiling screen that runs the entire length of the room. On her right against the opposite wall, is a tall, narrow screen encased in a black frame. The frame looks like a mirror hanging on a closet door for a final "clothes check" before stepping out. Considering the size and shape of her container, this third woman appears more rigid and constrained. She's not as clear as the others either, with some pixelation around her slightly hunched frame.

Looking back to the left, the youngest woman appears the most crisp. She has a 3-dimensional sense to her layers of clothing – down to the chunky threads of her sweater. She stands alongside a slightly older woman, who is the first to oblige on the recipe request.

"You have two problems, Ellede," she begins with an eyebrow

raised. "First, you need more ginger. Second, you're missing the secret ingredient," she concludes with a secretive smirk, raising her brow ever higher.

"And what's that Grandma?" Ellede responds, sensing she might soon get tweaked by the woman's sense of humor. She knows her feisty little quirks too well.

"Sage, baby, sage!" she says, twisting her hips in a little jig. Her ample top half bounces to the left, and her bottom lags behind somewhere on the right.

"Are you sure?" Ellede says, amused not just by her silly dance, but by the fact she never used sage in this particular recipe before.

"Believe me baby, I know," she stops her twisty dance, whipping a recipe card out of her plentiful cleavage to prove it.

Ellede rolls her eyes and chuckles under her breath. "Ok, ok," she calls out, conceding to Grandma's proof. She turns back to the stove and fishes around in a nearby cabinet.

"What other advice do you have for me today, Mothers?" Ellede calls over her shoulder while sprinkling sage into her soup. The preoccupation about her upcoming first day is back again to gnaw on her.

"Well in my day, you would do your hair this way," the feisty one chimes in again, waving her arm around her head. The movement transforms her hairdo into a dramatic night time look – her dark curls swept back into a low bun that she proudly turns to display to the others.

"Wait, wait," Mom calls out next to Grandma, hand on hip, observing. "That is so old-fashioned. Where are you headed, to the Senior Center social hour?" *Oh Mom* – always a source of sarcastic humor and practical critique. Mom's voice is clear and strong. Standing closest to Ellede, the sense in the room is that her voice is directly emanating from her mouth – coming across as the "nearest" to Ellede's ears. Whereas Grandma's voice sounds more diffuse.

"Oh that is so wrong," a much softer, faraway voice finally chimes in. "If you want to attract your man, you must do this," Great Grandma says in her picture frame, arguing with her progeny from across the room. She styles her hair into a white and blonde kind of bouffant, confidently raising her hunched head to show off her creation. Ellede turns and looks with a smile, always enjoying her hilarious, old-timey quips. This woman in the frame is relatively quiet in comparison to the others, but her echo from the past never disappoints. *Oh how I will always love my GG, Ellede warms inside.*

"Ok Moms – be quiet. I've had enough of your advice!" Ellede laughs with a sideways grin, knowing the conversation went far away from what she was looking for: a confident nudge into her new adventure. All the Mothers laugh in response to Ellede's audible *humph* as she goes back to the pot. Mom is the last to stop laughing, particularly enjoying the sarcasm gene she passed along to her daughter.

But Ellede really appreciates their advice, and they all know that. Whenever she needed, she could call upon them and talk about her greatest challenges. Their lifetimes of knowledge – captured and secure forever – became an invaluable asset in Ellede's life.

They may be departed, but never gone.

The only woman she knew in actual life was her mom, who died far too young at age 65. Yet as Mom's disease advanced, Ellede had no worries about her looming loss. There was no need. Grief was something she felt on occasion about other things, but never about death. And regrets? – none. *Mom is right here with me, always. How could I possibly be alone?* Ellede's heart is full and thankful. It mattered little that she only had her mom for 25 years "in life," and never even remembered her grandmother. With their Figments, she could know and experience so much more. She realizes she lives in a blessed time. And now, she is about to know everything from the inside – with her new job.

When Ellede pivots to the island to finish preparing a salad, she notices something in her peripheral vision and turns.

"Ah!!" announces a miniature version of Ellede, standing with her feet in A-frame like her mom, but with toes tipping up from the polished concrete floor. She strikes a groggy balance while holding a toy in her hand. Her bedraggled dark blond curls flow down her back, laying especially flat and kinked at the back of her head.

"Well good morning, little one!" Ellede smiles, walking over to smooth her child's bedhead. "Did you have a nice nap?"

"Hi sweet baby!" Grandma calls and waves from across the room. Mom next to her blows the child a kiss, hunching down and cooing in her direction, "Well I have never seen such a beauty. Look at you, little girl!" Not wanting to be one-upped, Grandma begins layering more praise on the child. "She's strong too. Tiny but mighty," Grandma corrects her daughter, tucking her chin.

As their continuous praise starts transforming into unsolicited parenting tips, Ellede begins tuning them out. She says to the child, "Baby, go play with Grandma GG while I finish our food." The bedhead at the back of her head is unphased by Ellede's touch as she guides her to the screen, hand firm against her upper back.

"Ellowen, come sit next to GG now," Great Grandma coos. The little girl sits with legs crossed, and GG follows suit on her screen, albeit with a slow and crooked movement down her picture frame. Finally, she arrives in a rigid and creaky seated position, legs folded together in front of her. She sweeps her hand around her head, changing her bouffant into a floppy straw hat. Taking off the hat, she pulls out a cat by the scruff of the neck, cups its behind, and places it with care on her folded legs. Mirroring GG, the child picks up her toy dog and places it on her lap as well. The joints of its hard carbon fiber body tap together as it comes to a rest. The dog's face, an oddly flat video representation of a Westie, looks up at the child with tongue hanging down in the opposite direction.

GG once again picks up the cat, facing it toward the child. "Bring him here, baby," she says.

Ellowen scoots closer and brings her robotic pet close to the screen as well. The dog and cat are so close, it's as if they are about to kiss across the plane of reality and screen.

With a puff of sparkle around GG's hands, suddenly the dog wiggles in the girl's hands. Surprised, Ellowen turns to look in its face, and sees the cat's face looking back at her. Soon after, the white skin of the robot transforms to a facsimile of GG's orange Tabby.

The child is delighted to see her dog turn to a cat, which wriggles free and pounces off sideways across the floor. Ellowen follows close behind, giggling, as GG watches in satisfaction at her work. "I haven't lost my touch yet in entertaining kids!" GG says to herself.

Across the room, Ellede has returned to her salad and the other Figments walk toward each other to interact. Mom casually walks past Grandma, leaving a strange transparent trail over her as she passes by. The movement degrades Grandma's clarity behind her, but soon the system catches up and she looks normal again.

Ellede notices how uncomfortable they look, wandering around the screen. She points her finger to a cozy seat in the room, then flicks her finger upward. A tiny menu projects up from her watch. She selects "replicate" with her raised finger, then drags the seat up to the screen. In an instant, a facsimile of the chair appears on the screen and Mom sits with a smooth grace. Then with the same finger, Ellede drags up a loveseat from the floor to the screen. Grandma looks behind her at the soft cushions, chirping, "Thanks Ellede." She sits down with less smooth definition than her daughter, and the two Mothers begin conversing with each other.

With Ellowen occupied with GG and everyone now comfortable, Ellede decides to get back to the matter at hand.

"Mom, Grandma – I'm starting my new job on Monday. What do you suggest?" Ellede begins.

"Ok, let me think," Mom replies, fishing around her cardigan pocket and materializing what looks like an old daily planner. "Ah, you are starting at Re-Life, is that correct?" she queries, referring to her book. Ellede concludes that it must be filled with her daily appointments.

"Yes, that's right Mom."

"Oooh," Grandma says, nodding her head in approval. She knows what Re-Life is. She knows that's where she "lives".

"Ok, I see a suggestion here about the office dress code," she continues from the book. "You must wear gray clothing, preferably a suit for your first day at least. The style of the attire is to ensure that everyone is equal. And that everyone is a blank slate. Hmm, that's interesting," she waxes on the esoteric last guideline.

"Ellede, you must know too – you are the best in your field," Grandma assures. "Just think about your education. Your past experience. This new job is completely within your capability."

"But Grandma, I'm feeling like this new role is at a higher level than I've ever accomplished before. I mean – can I do this?" Ellede stammers out the insecurities that bubbled in her all day.

"Of course you can. And you will," Mom looks up from her book and into her daughter's eyes. "In fact, feeling this way makes it even better   that way you can grow even more."

Ellede nods. They are confirming what she already knew. But

still – it felt so good to hear it from others.

Seeing that Ellede is more relaxed and satisfied, the Moms return to chit-chat with each other. Ellede looks on with interest. She knows they are interacting, but do they know they are "with" each other? Do they sense that they're here, in this room, with me? Do they "feel" the cushions underneath them? She knows enough about this technology to be dangerous. *But I'm going to need to find out more to be successful in this new job*, she concludes to herself. *I need to know everything.*

"Hey," another new arrival announces. In the same spot that Ellowen appeared, Ellede now sees a scraggly curly-headed man in pajama pants and a loose t-shirt. He has a warm sideways smile, growing more adorable by the second as he scratches his head. The Moms chime in again at the newcomer.

"Naps in the middle of the day?" Mom smiles, poking fun.

"Maybe for the baby girl but not for the husband too!" Grandma laughs.

"But it's Saturday!" Jonathan semi-pouts. They didn't know he earned that sleep after his software deployment all-nighter.

Ellede snickers, nearly an incredulous snort, drinking in her sweet man's broad smile. Salad finished, she passes by Jonathan, planting a soft kiss on his cheek.

"Ok dear Mothers, I've heard enough for one day!" she says with a smile and wink to her beloved. She begins the monitor shutdown by tapping a panel on the wall and whisks the little girl away from GG's picture frame. "Bye GG," the girl babbles, waving over her mother's shoulder. GG's eyes twinkle back at her.

"Ok Ellede, good luck in your new job!" they all interject with similar sentiments in their own distinct ways.

As Jonathan walks toward the dinner table, Mom stands and squeezes her arms around her as if to throw him a virtual hug. He moves his fingers into a heart shape as he passes by and uses his palm to push it into the screen. Mom drops into a receiver's pose, grabbing the floating heart in her hands with a wide grin. "Goodnight son," she speaks as she fades away.

The screens wane into a neutral gray. Their texture and color is indiscernible from a normal wall. Jonathan busies himself with setting up his daughter's highchair at the table.

"Did you sleep ok? How did the deployment go?" Ellede asks him, hugging Ellowen in her arms and kissing her head. The child hangs on to her robot pet by the ear with her tiny vice grip fingers.

"Difficult. The security patching never seems to end," Jonathan replies. "It's getting worse. I suspect you'll get an earful when you walk in the door on Monday," he flashes a sideways smile, but this time with a tinge of sarcasm.

"Hmm," Ellede ponders his familiar refrain. He works at Re-Life too – and she's heard his stories. Some situations seemed to teeter on the brink of losing control of aspects of the system. She has no doubt this *will* come up as part of her job too.

Jonathan's role provided a line of sight into Re-Life that few could leverage. As his position grew more intense by the minute, Ellede listened carefully. Why should she accept a job there and enter such a seemingly volatile world too?

The fact remained that every risk was successfully mitigated. Not just during Jonathan's deployment last night, but for *decades* now, Jonathan and his team's top-notch work made it so. She has every confidence that the world they live in now – *that her daughter will live in* – offers great rewards. Rewards that were not possible without Re-Life. Rewards that outweigh the risks every time. It's a no brainer. How could she *not* be a part of that?

Highchair ready, she passes the child into Jonathan's arms. He places her in the chair, then deposits her animal friend on the floor. It proceeds to swerve in and out of the chair legs, entertaining itself by rubbing against them. But instead of freeing loose cat hair, its carbon fiber just *tap-tap-taps* against the metal legs. With Ellowen entranced by her pet's new behavior, Ellede and Jonathan proceed to carry plates and bowls for their early evening meal into the dining area.

"Well, I bet you're doing great," Ellede breaks her reverie. "No matter what happens from a security perspective, you'll address it. I'm just sorry you have to do so many all-nighters!"

"Ha – me too," he chuckles. "But at least I can handle the deployments from here," tipping his head toward his home office setup tucked in the corner of the room.

Ah yes, what a blessing. She can't imagine him going out at night in the crime-riddled city. She has so many blessings, never taking them for granted. The sweet smell of the simmering stew, the warmth of her sweatshirt, her love, her family, her job. Even this place: how lucky they are to be here, in this apartment owned and paid for by Re-Life. They earned that added perk given Jonathan's (and now Ellede's) employment.

Granted, Ellowen's bedroom was more like a closet than anything. But she was still small. It is enough for now. The girl had room to roam in their large living area instead – a combination kitchen, dining, living, and office space. Ellede and Jonathan's favorite part sat in the middle – a two-sided wood-burning fireplace, accessible from both the living area and their adjacent bedroom. It's a luxury available to only a few now. This facet of nature stood out at the heart of an otherwise sterile block of concrete and screens. The entire place was windowless, except for one small gap at the top of their bedroom wall.

But that was the price to ensure security these days. Without this concrete fortress with one window high off the street, they couldn't work here in town. Re-Life knew that, so this kind of subsidized benefit to employees became the norm.

Still on rare days, sunlight opened the gray sky. It spilled across their bed, warming their hearts and bodies. And the hearth offered a rare, delightful indulgence. The scent of burning wood brought back something of the primal and grounded spirit. Of an earlier time... of *home*.

As Ellede ponders working for the same entity as her husband, she acknowledges that his employment *alone* is well compensated. They were allowed access to software and equipment that others could only dream of, due to Jonathan's long tenure at Re-Life. They had a *friends and family* discount (*literally*), so they never missed out. She did not take their privileges as early adopters for granted. And now, she could not picture her life without her Mothers. They were her heart... her soul lifeblood. She felt again at home, in the deepest way.

As they return to the table with the stew, the adjacent screen transforms the plain wall into a new window. It reveals a sandy coastline flanked by blowing, gauzy curtains. A place preserved forever in their virtual domain, that they may never see in real life.

Ghana... how beautiful. And apropos! She takes care to scoop up a more peanutty portion of the synchronous stew for little Ellowen, and reserves the spicy peppers for her and Jonathan.

Ellede finally sits, relaxing into her first bite. *Oh yes. Thanks Grandma for the "sage" advice.*

"Mmm delicious," Jonathan soon articulates what's in her mind, savoring his first bite too.

"But you are the tastiest of all," Ellede responds, thinking about the sweetness of his cheek on her lips moments before. She gazes into his stunning, midnight blue eyes. *Oh, how my heart blooms*. Looking at him, she glows with a sphere of sparklers deep in her belly.

Young Ellowen remains oblivious to the love emanating from her parents at the other end of the table. Instead, she enjoys her meal. She reaches to the salad, selecting baby carrots and marching them around her plate as if they were tiny people. Looking down at her cat, she remembers her fun with GG. Her parents remain equally oblivious to her musings, engrossed instead in their conversation.

"I overheard what you all were talking about as I came in," Jonathan says. "Don't worry. You will do great."

"Why, thank you my sweet," Ellede responds in a bemused tone, laced with extra sugar to amplify her contentment.

"Besides, I know you can be a hard ass when you need to be," he grins.

"Ha!!!" she exclaims, taking an aggressive chomp off her plantain chip. It's true. Of the two, she is the outgoing and outspoken one. She's an extrovert – friendly and able to speak to anyone with ease. Drawing people out of their shells was her secret sauce. It's what made her great at her last job and will propel her into her new one: Director of Public Relations, Advertising, and Corporate Communications.

Whereas Jonathan was strong as a granite block – introspective, analytical, smart as a tack. Technical in his approach, and adept in his execution. He made everything work. Still, he exemplified empathy at work, connecting people who would otherwise never mesh. And at home, he exuded tenderness – always loving to Ellede and their daughter. This was his magic. And that is why Ellede and Jonathan made an excellent team.

"What can you tell me about orientation?" Ellede probes, still smiling. Jonathan, a long-time DevOps Director at the company, knew the ins and outs. In fact, she learned about the opportunity through her husband. In a way, he pilfered her from her previous company just by letting her know about the position. Her solid career history sealed the deal. Once she conducted her interview, the company's decision was clear: her offer came in the same day.

She took her time deciding to accept. The circumstances were rather unclear about the departure of the previous employee who filled her role. Intel was sketchy, even to Jonathan – a stalwart insider. Just that there were "differences".

"Well, everyone goes through The Hall first," Jonathan begins answering Ellede's question. "Then I'm thinking you'll meet with the Senior VP and CEO. They'll promptly throw you into the deep end of the pool," he pokes at her again with a smile.

"Of course." She expected the latter part. But his unfamiliar terminology left her wondering aloud, "What is The Hall?"

"Oh, you'll find out," he's elusive, but she can tell he's excited. She's pleased to see that twinkle of anticipation still in his eye. In all their talks, Ellede knows one thing. Jonathan is proud of his work, but he's a hardened Re-Life stalwart. He has seen some things. Even his side of the family was, let's say, less embracing of this technology. She honestly didn't understand why. He didn't discourage them, of course. But he did share some realities with them that only he could see.

Ellede, on the other hand, was open to listening and weighing her options accordingly. She was a realist to her core. But she embraced the technology from the beginning and reaped its benefits. Zooming ahead to today, her attitude remains positive. She's as optimistic as any new hire would be on the threshold of starting a tremendous adventure. Now that she's made her choice, she was all-in.

"What do you think will be the hardest part?" Ellede queries, interested in drawing Jonathan out more.

"Ellede, you know how I feel. What we do – and now what you will do – is nothing short of miraculous. Magnificent, even. But when it goes bad, well, it…" He trails off, a shadow falling across his expression.

"There are dangers you haven't seen yet," he continues. "I don't want to discourage you. But just…" he pauses again, trying to find the right words to balance optimism with caution. "Just learn as much as you can. And be alert."

Alert? What does that mean?

"Jonathan, I think it will be fine. Just look at what we have here! I can't picture our lives any differently," Ellede assures, realizing that it's her turn to balance him. She doesn't see these supposed *dangers*. She is a living, breathing example of the *good* that Figments brought to society. There was zero downside to having her Mothers around.

I mean, if he or his parents had their way, would they prevent Ellowen from knowing her family? What would she stand to lose in her life without access to their wisdom and companionship? Her mood darkens just thinking about it.

Ugh, she recoils internally, trying to shake her line of thinking by shifting to a broader gear. *Ellowen will have access to her Figment Mothers – to their generations of love and guidance, helping to steer her life, just as they did mine. I'll do anything to ensure that.*

*If everything was just like this, for everyone in the world, then how could it be bad? Nothing is ever easy. But I'm in for the greater good. It **is** "magnificent."*

"Happy wife, happy life," he says, watching her wheels turn. His sideways grin returns as she softens, and he goes back to savor his last bite.

They finish their meal in silence, listening to soothing wind chimes and watching the beachy curtains blow in breezes found only in the screen's faraway place. Relaxed, they rise to clear the table. She resolves to herself: *I know what I'm getting into. And it's worth it to work for the most consequential employer in the world.*

Jonathan watches her pick up the leftover stew. In an unexpected rush, he embraces her from behind. He is taller than her, enough to make her feel small and protected in his arms. His touch shifts her focus back to grace, erasing what's left of her nerves as his body presses into her back. She melts into him.

He runs a hand up her legging, over her hip, under her sweatshirt, and to her lower belly. He feels the firm softball there, just beginning to form. He senses the sturdiness of her stance, her bones. Just like this place, a refuge of safety, her body itself is changing to a fortress under his hands.

He buries his face in her hair, breathing her in, feeling the need to shield her from his intense look. Because now, he knows that he protects something more – as something else flutters there.

In a few moments, her hand joins his on her belly. They look to the screen, out to sea lapping tan sand, listening to birds on the breeze.

The story continues in the forthcoming novel,
FIGMENTS (THE RE-LIFE STORY: BOOK ONE).
For more information, stay connected at www.CarisaHK.com.

my people

Rose Pulford

By blood and by choice
These are my people
The ones who fill my soul
Who hold me close when all else fails
These are my people
The one who fill my memories
They are my family

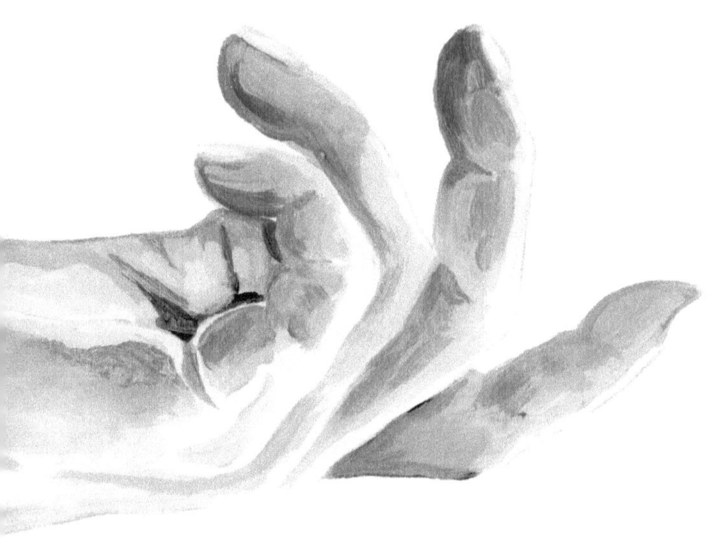

romance

cycling romance

Amanda Kennedy

Carly stepped out of her car and pulled at the waistband of her new yoga pants. They were, in fact, a size too small as the salesgirl had hinted. As much as she tried to still fit into the size she wore in her thirties, she couldn't deny that she was no longer comfortable in a medium. Oh well. She pulled them up higher, feeling the squeeze of the tummy control feature. Trying to appear casual, she swept her eyes over the large parking lot. Despite the tight squeeze of the slimming spandex, her stomach did a flip when she spotted his black Jeep. Not his usual spot, she noted. Grabbing her gym bag from the backseat, she closed the door and attempted what she hoped was an effortlessly cool stride up to the glass doors of the health club.

Paul walked around the second-floor track that encircled the health club's fitness center below. It offered a view of everything going on in the gym beneath him, but most importantly, it looked over the parking lot and the club's front doors. Each time he reached the front end of the track, he paused to tighten his shoelaces or stretch his back while scanning the parking lot through the expansive wall of windows. Rounding the track for the fourth time, he knelt to re-tie his shoes, and looked up to see her walking up to the front doors. New yoga pants, he noticed, appreciating the view. Having nothing to do with his cardiovascular activity, Paul's heart rate increased and he got up to hurry to the stairs and reach the stationary bikes before she did.

Carly swiped her membership card at the front desk and headed straight to the women's locker room. After stashing her purse and sunglasses in a locker and tucking the key into her too tight pants pocket, she stopped at the wall of mirrors to evaluate her reflection. The loose tank top hid her midsection insecurities, but left her upper arms with nowhere to hide. She turned and flexed the way she'd seen younger women do while they took the mirror selfies destined for social media posts. Not too bad she admitted, giving credit to the rowing machine. Turning back to face the mirror, she frowned at her too tight ponytail. Her mother had once told her it made her face look big. She pulled it out to redo and teased a few strands loose, then turned away from the mirrors to enter the fitness center.

Paul straddled his usual stationary bike, which happened to be two machines over from her usual bike. Exercise bikes were not really his thing. He'd tried them out a few times when he started coming here but decided to give it up when his knees complained after only five minutes of pedaling. He had been declaring himself officially done with cycling just as she came in one day and sat two bikes over from him. It was the scent of vanilla that turned his gaze, but when he saw her reach down and pull a piece of toilet paper from the bottom of her shoe and mutter *'oh shit'* under her breath, he had to choke back his laugh and ended up staying for the entire duration of her cycling session.

Since then, he'd become an expert at lowering the tension and slowing his speed to give the impression he was working harder than he was. While he waited for her to come out of the women's room, he followed the sound of one of the club's trainers, an intense woman with bulging biceps and an orange tan. She was on all fours, loudly coaxing an elderly man in a plank to HOLD! Paul watched the man shake with the effort until his attention was drawn to the women's locker room door opening.

Carly stopped at the water fountain to fill her bottle and pull at the hem of her shirt. She was glad of the excuse to delay her walk across the gym floor. Walking across the room always made her feel uncomfortably exposed, even though she knew no one was checking out a frumpy, middle-aged woman. To avoid looking in his direction as she walked over to the row of stationary bikes, she tried to look interested in what grueling torture the club's trainer was putting someone through. Today's victim was a man shaking in a plank.

Sensing her approach before he could see her, Paul looked down and fiddled with the settings on his bike to better resist the urge to watch her walk up. To be honest, he felt he was ready to increase the tension of the machine. His quads had gained definition he hadn't seen since his thirties and his knees were much improved and hardly hurt anymore. When she reached her bike, he pulled his stomach in and sat up taller in the seat. He considered whether they were at that place yet where they could acknowledge each other's presence with a nod or a casual smile and *'Hi'*. Paul chanced turning his head towards her.

Carly climbed onto the bike two machines away from him. Since the first time she saw him here and had worked up the courage to try cycling just for the chance to sit near him, she'd tried to time her visits to coincide with his. It turned out to be easier than she imagined, and she began to worry she looked like a stalker. Honestly, she didn't even like cycling. She had noticed, though, her butt was more toned. She set the bike to her preferred speed and tension, proud to have learned how to work the thing. Once she began pedaling, she tried to imagine talking to him. It had been a month, she reasoned. He had to have noticed her by now. She tried out a few possibilities in her head. *How's it going? Nice shorts. Do you come here often?* She bit back a laugh at the terrible pick-up lines.

The corners of her mouth turned up in a smile and Paul just managed to stop himself from smiling in return like a creep. If he was going to say something it would have to be now, he told himself. Before she caught him looking at her. He searched his mind for something witty. *We can't keep meeting like this.* Oh, God, no. He cringed and looked away. The intense trainer was leading his client through a floor exercise. She ran alongside him, shouting words of encouragement while he performed lunges with a kettlebell weight held high over his head.

Carly thought she felt his eyes on her and risked a sideways look only to feel disappointed that he wasn't looking at her at all, but at the trainer. She followed his gaze and watched the poor guy struggle to keep a weight over his head while he alternated stepping forwards and backwards. The trainer squatted low next to him and yelled, "Do it! You got this! Come on!" Her words traveled across the gym all the way to Carly as though personally addressed to her. It was just the push she needed, and she acted before she lost her nerve.

"Excuse me," she said, slowing the pedals to a stop. She pointed to the bike between them and asked, "Is this seat taken?"

finally

K.I. Runyon

The deadline had passed an hour ago and Logan still hadn't written a single word since James fucking Macon had walked into the coffee shop. Logan had multiple passive aggressive Slack messages asking where his most recent analysis was on the new vice-presidential pick but all he could do was sit there and panic.

Life was generally okay for Logan. He loved his job. He wrote for one of the best up-and-coming political sites in the country even though he'd only graduated from college two years ago.

He'd figured out a way to make money on his history degree in spite of his father's worries and he was living in a city where being gay was like the grass being green. No one cared. It was part of the way of the world and it wasn't a decision that required any announcements. All in all, Chicago treated him well.

Especially on a day like today. The coffee shop's large bay windows let the sun stream in while they played one of Logan's favorite John Mayer albums and the chatter around him was the perfect amount of background noise not to be a distraction.

One of the best baristas in the city had made Logan a grade A cortado to sip on while he wrote. He had plenty of primary source material and he had a genuine interest in writing the article. Regardless, nothing was working. Logan couldn't stop glancing across the room.

Sitting there casually in the shop was James Macon. The man Logan had been in love with for six long years. James had said hello to Logan in an economics class on day two of freshman year at North-western and that had been it.

The young guy from Texas on a football scholarship had had the biggest megawatt smile and sunniest disposition Logan had ever witnessed. It hadn't hurt that in addition to being attractive, James was funny, caring, and more obsessed with anime than Logan.

A group of cheerleaders entered the shop and provided enough cover for Logan to spend a long moment studying James. He chatted with a man Logan didn't recognize, beaming and sipping on what looked like a latte.

James wore dark blue jeans and a black t-shirt that stretched across his broad chest. His dark brown wavy hair was styled differently than the last time Logan had seen him at graduation. Buzzed on the sides and long on top, the haircut of the times.

His golden-brown eyes were framed by new laugh lines and he had an ease about him that hadn't been there in school when he'd been the star quarterback. The man across from James was an attractive blonde who'd come straight from the gym.

Logan looked down at his shaking hands and pretended to type. He didn't dare linger too long; he didn't want to appear as if he was staring, or pining. He'd allowed himself a quick look whenever James got up to grab a napkin or refill his water glass. That was it.

Logan needed to leave, but he was worried that might attract attention. Well, James' attention, that was. While they'd once been best friends, they hadn't spoken since graduation because of Logan's actions.

He still woke up in the middle of the night in cold sweats, the secondhand embarrassment of the memory of what happened a pressing weight on his chest.

Logan sipped his drink and took a deep breath. All he needed to do was keep reading his notes from last night's campaign stop long enough for James and his friend to leave so Logan could get back to work.

A throaty, and very sexy laugh sounded from across the cafe, mocking Logan's honest intentions. *Damn it, James.* Here Logan was, having moved on, well mostly, when the man who inspired the majority of his sexual fantasies reappeared.

Was it a sign or a cruel twist of fate? That the man he'd confessed his love to and who'd shot him down immediately after was only ten feet away. Maybe this was the universe telling him he was strong enough to handle this.

He could say hello like a normal person and ask James how he'd been. And then walk away like it wouldn't shatter the heart that he'd spent a painstaking amount of time putting back together.

Fuck this. The universe was wrong. This was pathetic. Logan threw back his drink and packed up his things faster than a sorority girl taking Jello shots. It was time to get the hell out of there.

Pulling off his sweatshirt and stuffing it in his bag so he wouldn't overheat walking on his way home, Logan kept his head down and left the coffee mug, making sure James wouldn't see him if he happened to look up.

Logan had walked about half a block and was pulling out his phone to text his sister about the day's events when he heard someone calling for him.

"Logan, wait up!"

It was James. Logan froze, uncertain how to proceed. Should he pretend like he hadn't heard him? Or turn around and act surprised? God, this was so embarrassing. *Be cool. Be cool.*

"Logan!" James called again. Logan pocketed his phone and turned with a bright, fake smile. James reached him, slightly out of breath, his hair mussed from the wind.

"Oh, James? Wow, what a surprise. How are you?" Logan asked, wondering briefly what happened to the man James had been sitting with.

James grinned, gaining a twinkle in those beautiful chocolate eyes of his. His breathing calmed and he stood up straight. He must've really been sprinting. Part of one side of his shirt had ridden up, showing that line that meant a man was in really fucking good shape. Logan felt the blood rush to his head and tiny little black spots dotted his vision.

"Liar. I know you saw me," James said, but it was without any heat. He was teasing Logan. Logan's neck itched and he felt his cheeks burn. He looked down at the sidewalk.

"I didn't want to interrupt," Logan said.

A warm, calloused finger curled under Logan's chin and lifted his head until they were looking at each other. Logan was certain his entire face was scarlet by this point.

Logan thought James would let go and step back but when they made eye contact, they both lingered, not saying a word. Logan would be the one to look away, in one more second, after he'd filed away all the little details that his memories had started forgetting.

There was the scar under James' left eyebrow from a fight he'd gotten into their sophomore year during the game against their school's biggest rival. The white line under his lip from the car accident he got into when he was five. The mole on the right side of his chin.

He'd missed him so damned much. But he had to keep himself removed. James didn't feel that way. Correction, James didn't like men. Which Logan very much did.

"No, Max, no!" a voice interrupted the moment, and Logan fell forward with a sudden force.

"What the –"

"I'm so sorry," a kind looking, older woman said from several feet away as James caught Logan against his chest.

A large golden retriever with an untethered leash had jumped up on Logan's back, shoving him forward. James grabbed Logan around the waist with one arm, while he spun him to the side and grabbed the dog's collar with his other hand.

Logan gulped, realizing the situation. They were both over six feet tall and fit so it was no small feat for James to catch him and take control of the situation. It was also really fucking hot.

God damn. Of course it had to be a day when Logan was already sweating from the heat that this would happen. He could feel the moisture gathering at his temples as the situation evolved.

The older woman in athletic gear reached them then.

"I am so sorry," she repeated. "I'm watching my daughter's dog. I didn't know how strong he was." She grabbed the leash.

"You okay?" James asked Logan. Logan nodded, not at all concerned about the dog when James Macon had him pressed up against his body and had yet to let go. James smiled at the woman.

"No problem, ma'am. Have a good day," James said.

The woman went on her way and Logan tried to step away from James, to give himself some space, but James refused to let go. Logan tugged again.

"You're not running away again," James growled. Logan's eyes widened.

"What are you talking about?" he asked.

"Can we talk?" James asked, loosening his hold somewhat. His eyes blinked several times and he lost a bit of his usual swagger. "Somewhere private maybe?"

At that moment, the rest of the world filtered in and Logan realized they were standing in the middle of a crowded street hip to hip and people were having to walk around them as they rushed to their destinations. Logan swallowed, his spit getting stuck in his throat and tasting like sand.

"Sure," he said. It was meant to sound casual, cool, but it came out shaky.

James flashed his signature grin in return and Logan cursed on the inside. What could James possibly have to say? Maybe he'd want to be friends, saying they could work around Logan's feelings.

Ugh. That would be worse. *Friends.* Who wanted to be friends with a dude who looked like that? Logan wanted to marry this man and somehow have his babies. He didn't want to gossip about all the girls James wanted to bang.

"Come on, I know a place," James said, letting go of Logan and gesturing at him to turn down the street. Logan followed obediently. It'd always been that way with them.

Besides running away and ghosting James and their friendship after the debacle of two years ago, he'd never once defied James. In fact, he got a little thrill from listening to him. And maybe that was the problem.

They found a small park that Logan had never been to and James gestured for them to sit on an empty bench. They took up the entire seat. James cleared his throat.

"Why?" he asked.

Logan frowned.

"Why what?" Logan asked.

"Why did you block me and completely disappear from my life?" James asked.

"Fuck, going for the jugular, huh?" Logan joked.

"Well, what do you want me to say? The man I was in love with told me he loved me first and while I was processing how fucking amazing the news was – but how I didn't know what to say because I wasn't out yet – he ran away like a fucking coward and I never saw him again."

Logan tried to speak but no words came out. He tried again. And again. James waited, ever patient.

"I thought," Logan started in a whisper, "I thought you were gathering up the courage to reject me. You didn't look happy at all."

"I wasn't. I was ecstatic. And also a little terrified. Ok. A lot terrified," he said. He clasped his hands in front of him and rubbed the inside of his palm with his thumb.

"It wasn't just about how I felt or how you felt. I knew it would be making a statement. I mean, I was already gaining a lot of attention for having declined to join the NFL draft so I could go to medical school. The press coverage and what they'd say about us was playing out in my head. I was angry that it would take away from us, from the moment. That someone might tarnish the real story. You know, the one about two best friends who'd gotten lucky enough to fall for one another?"

"Oh fuck," Logan said, breathing out a long, uneven breath. He ran his hands through his long dark hair and looked down at the ground. James' words began to register. "You loved me?" Logan squeaked out.

"Well, unfortunately for me, it's not past tense. Not yet anyway," James said in a sardonic tone.

Logan's head whipped up and his jaw dropped. James gave him what was intended to be a smug smirk, but it lacked the confidence needed to pull it off.

Logan didn't let any more thoughts get in the way of what he wanted. He leaned in and crushed his lips to James. James groaned and pulled Logan closer, James' hands tightening around Logan's head and his back.

"Fucking. Finally." James said, each word punctuated by a kiss.

Logan answered with his own tightening of his fist in James's shirt, feeling the words in his soul. Fucking finally indeed.

favor the brave

Allison Matalone

My stomach rolls down, down, to the pit of my abdomen and twists nauseously as the plane rises. I could kick myself; I can't believe I forgot gum. I mime chewing in an effort to balance the pressure in my ears. I hate flying.

Not for the first time, I wonder why I'm doing this? I haven't seen Derek in nearly six years. After graduation, he got into a writing seminar at Oxford and ended up staying. Our friendship since has been based on sharing memes on Facebook, following him on Instagram, and being his first subscriber on TikTok. His fish-out-of-water shorts went viral two years ago. And since then, suddenly, he has an agent and people are writing articles about him. And now, he has a meeting in LA about optioning a book.

This is the closest he's been to me in six years and I didn't even hesitate to book plane tickets. The only problem is he doesn't know I'm coming.

"Nervous about flying?"

I glance over at the woman next to me and immediately still my hands which had been unconsciously flexing. She looks like one of my aunts, plump with streaks of gray in her black hair and warm brown eyes behind glasses. She has a tablet in her lap.

"Uh, no, I mean yes, kind of, not the flying part, I'm going to meet someone?" Why it came out as a question is beyond me.

"It's this guy –," I can feel my face get hot.

She puts the tablet into the front pocket next to emergency landing guides and barf bags. "Tell me all about him."

"Well…" I begin and think about freshman year almost a decade ago.

Derek had sat beside me in Theatre Appreciation freshman year and we had bonded over a hatred for the overachiever who sat up front and *Romeo and Juliet*, which we both felt was overdone, and trite.

"I mean seriously," I began as we gathered our bags. "Romeo was infatuated with someone else."

"Roselyn," he supplied.

"Yeah, and suddenly he's in love with Juliet?" I slung my bag over my shoulder, "It's utterly ridiculous. He just wanted to sex her up. And what is so romantic about suicide? Nothing."

We start walking to the doors. Derek shrugged, grinning. "Well, I think it's the concept of dying for love."

"But, wouldn't it be more romantic to live in love." I hold the door open.

"I think that Shakespeare did an injustice with the story. I mean the original story has the two lovers growing up side by side, separated by a physical wall as well as the emotional wall of their parents' hate." He paused, running a hand through his hair.

"Of course," He continues, "they do die in the end, there's a lioness and a dropped cloak, and one thing leads to another, and Pyramus kills himself and then Thisbe herself, but…" he saw my smiling face and trailed off, his face going red.

"You're a closeted literature nerd, aren't you?" I teasingly accused.

He sighed and dropped his head. "Guilty."

I leaned over and stage-whispered, "At least Ovid's story has a point, I mean, come on, the color of mulberries is like so important. But I'm partial to Pygmalion myself."

"Obsessive?"

"Obsessive? I think you're thinking about Narcissus, who was obsessed with himself."

"Compared to Pygmalion, who was so obsessed with a statue he built himself, he fell in love with it."

I waved my hand to disregard his statement. "She eventually became real, so it all worked out."

He laughed, "So is only Roman poetry? Because I have a lot of thoughts about Gilgamesh."

"Don't we all."

"So best friend in college, and when did you know you were in love with him?"

I groan and put my hands over my eyes. Was I that obvious that even this stranger could tell? "I didn't even realize until he was off to Oxford for a writing seminar."

"And when was that?"

I peek out from between my fingers. "Six years ago?" Once again my statement comes out as a question.

"Honey," She put her hand on her chest, and I could hear the unsaid 'bless your heart' "What have you been doing all this time?"

I put my hands down and sit up straight. "In my defense, I didn't want to, ya know, profess my love with an ocean between us, and then he ended up staying in England. And AND," I nearly shout the last word, because I can see her mouth opening to criticize. "I was going to go see him and hopefully tell him, but Covid shut the world down and then I lost my job. So obviously that didn't happen."

"And now he's back stateside."

"Yes."

She pats my hand, "You've got this."

The intercom chimes and the pilot announces that the temperature is a balmy 78 degrees and sunny as we begin our descent. I look out the window and see LA.

I don't think I have this, but I don't want to contradict the very nice lady who has let me ramble on about Derek for the better part of this plane ride.

I see my face in the window pane and I try to reassure my doubtful, hesitant reflection. You can do this. You will do this.

It's remarkably easy to stalk a TikTok star. The most recent posts he's been tagged in leave a trail of breadcrumbs for me to follow. The latest one has him buying a Lychee Bubble Tea at a place called Best-Teas.

I leave Best-teas, sans a tea, there is no time to hydrate, He was here just ten minutes ago. Leaning against the pedestrian crossing pole, I check all the socials for a hint of where he could be.

I could just message him, but there's something romantic and dramatic about finding him in the wild. I decided if I can't find him by this evening, I'll shoot him a DM. I pull up Google Maps and start scanning the various stores nearby and there not two blocks away is Babylon Books. Derek never stopped being a literature nerd. The walk signal flashes and I hurry across the street.

Babylon Books is almost hidden, squashed between a CBD shop and a Juice bar. The lettering on the windows is cracked from years of exposure to the elements. I pull open the door and step in.

I've always loved the smell of books, usually I find it calming, but right now it's doing little to stop the pounding of my heart and blood rushing in my ears. He has to be here. Right?

I scan the signs hanging above each aisle, and head for the last one Classical Literature. I round the corner and there he is with his back to me. Floppy black hair, squashed under a baseball cap, and part of his Gilgamesh tattoo where it spiraled around his upper arm:

WE WILL NOT FEAR

I take a deep breath, ready to say something until he turns and the words stick in my throat.

Jamie?" His blue blue eyes widen and his face breaks into a grin.

"Hi," I do an awkward wave with my hand and I'm not quite sure how to stand. I've gone over this meeting again and again, and never am I just frozen and unable to form words.

He rushes forward to embrace me in a crushing hug and suddenly I can breathe again and I bring my arms up to return his enthusiasm. .

"Hey stranger. Of all the bookstores," He starts.

"In all the cities," I finish.

He lets me go and steps back, "What are you doing here?"

"Stalking this TikTok star. Maybe you've heard of him.."

"Shut up. God, this is so ironic, I literally just bought a ticket to Denver." He flashed his phone screen at me as proof. Flight details for a flight on Sunday to Denver.

"You were coming to Denver?"

"Of course! Couldn't be stateside without seeing my best mate."

"Best mate? Oh, no. Have you gone native?"

He laughs and takes his cap off to smooth his hair. "Shit, I haven't practiced this enough."

"Practiced what?"

"I kind of thought I had two more days to work up to this. Um." He shoves a book he was holding at me. "I came in here to buy this for you." I take the book, there's no title on the front, I open up to the first page:

THE METAMORPHOSES OF OVID.

I look up at him and I can see the same hesitation, the same uncertainty.

"Fortune and love," I say and close the distance, breathing in his scent, warm and comforting with a touch of lychee. I cup his face, his eyes are bright, mouth parted and I press my lips to his.

the worst day

Brooke Thompson

I picked the wrong day to wear open-toe heels. Icy needles pricked my toes as I trudged to my car; rain splattering against my umbrella. I shivered inside my thin gray jacket, wishing I could at least put my hand in the pockets. My fingers were numb from the dreary November weather.

My foot slipped out from underneath me and I crashed to the ground, banging my knees on the wet asphalt. Small pebbles dug into my hands as I tried lifting myself off the ground. My left foot started to wobble, threatening to send me back down.

My heart sank when I noticed the heel had broken off inside a small crack in the pavement. "As if today could get any worse," I muttered, limping to the car. "These shoes were my favorites." I wiped my eyes and extended my arms for balance, trying to ignore how much my knees and palms stung from the fall. At least the car was close.

I unlocked the car door and tossed my umbrella onto the floor of the passenger side. As I settled into the driver's seat, my phone buzzed against my leg. I pulled the phone out of my pocket to see Ryder's photo lighting up the screen.

Though we had been together for two years, butterflies still fluttered inside my stomach whenever he called. I slid the green phone icon across his profile picture - a cute selfie of him holding my dog Abby - and answered the phone.

"Hey, babe," he said. "How are you today?"

"Oh, everything is great," I remarked before turning the key in the ignition. The car shuddered as the engine rumbled to life. "I had the best day at work,"

I set the phone down as it connected to the car's Bluetooth. "That bad, huh?" he said, his voice echoing through the speakers.

Goosebumps spread across my arms as warm air flowed from the vents. "I was hoping to leave on time today," I said, "but my boss made me stay late to write an emergency blog."

My boyfriend gasped. "You work for a pajama company. What could they need an 'emergency blog' for?"

I glanced over my shoulder before backing the car out of its parking spot. "Marketing is doing a last-minute flannel campaign and wanted a thousand-word blog explaining why it's perfect to wear in winter."

"What happened to the campaign on animal-themed pajamas?" he asked, trying to talk over the faint pop music playing in the background. "That sounded fun."

The rain picked up as I steered the car onto the street. "Who knows, honestly. By the way, when do you get back from your trip again?"

Someone was shouting in the background as Ryder spoke. I couldn't make out what they were saying, but they sounded angry. "I get back Sunday evening. Hey, do you mind if I get off? I'm in line for food."

The light up ahead turned red. I tapped the brakes. "Yeah, that's fine. I need to focus on driving anyway."

I hung up the phone and leaned back in my seat, listening to the rain beat against the windows. Three more days without Ryder. *Why couldn't his job have training here?* I thought, staring at the cars zooming by. *Why did they have to send him to California?*

The light turned green. I made a left to get on the highway, only to see dozens of red tail lights illuminating the road. Sirens wailed in the distance as red and blue beams flashed.

My fists clenched around the steering wheel. I screamed. "Just what I needed! A fucking wreck." My normal fifteen-minute commute turned into a forty-five-minute drive as cars crammed into the left lane.

It was dark by the time I made it home. The glowing lights of the apartment complex greeted me as my car settled into its parking spot under the carport.

I pulled my jacket tight around me and raced to my apartment, grateful it was on the first floor. I shoved the key into the rusty lock and jiggled the knob. The lock refused to move. "No," I said, twisting and pulling helplessly on the door handle. "Don't tell me it's broken."

My phone buzzed inside my pocket. I yanked it out to see who the caller was. It was Ryder again. Wedging the phone between my cheek and shoulder, I answered it.

"Hey, cutie!" Ryder said, "Are you back at the apartment yet?"

I tried inserting the key into the lock again. "Kind of. This stupid door won't open."

"Did you try pushing against the door then turning the lock?" Ryder asked. "I know sometimes it gets stuck."

"Yes, I did," I growled. "I thought you said maintenance fixed it."

"No, I said they put a work order in."

I beat my fist against the door and it swung open. "Finally! It only took a million years."

Slamming the door behind me, I stomped into the apartment. The sound echoed through the empty space. I tore off my jacket and threw it onto the couch. My eyes glanced to Abby's dog bed in the corner; only a threadbare tennis ball remained.

"Callie?" Ryder said. "Callie, are you there?"

I shook my head. "Oh, yeah, sorry. What were you saying?"

A cold drop of water plopped against my nose. I tilted my head back and noticed a dark stain on the ceiling. Water dripped down into a big puddle on the floor.

I let out a frustrated sigh. "We have a leak."

"Maintenance should've fixed that when they were here last week," Ryder remarked.

"Well, they didn't." I flung open the closet door to get the mop bucket and flinched as a roach skittered by my foot. *Looks like maintenance also forgot to spray for bugs.*

Ryder's voice sounded garbled as I picked up the plastic bucket. "Hang on. I'm in the closet." I stepped back into the living room and positioned the bucket underneath the leak.

"It's so weird how the closet gets no rec-" Ryder was cut off by a loud crackling noise. The phone beeped in my ear. "No! Not again!" I exclaimed, staring down at the words *Call Failed* across the top of the screen.

I threw my phone on my couch and stomped into the kitchen to grab paper towels for the puddle. I glanced over at the crockpot on the counter. A feeling of dread crept over me. *Did I remember to turn that on this morning?* I couldn't smell the roast.

The crockpot's white cord was plugged into the wall. The dial was set on low, but I couldn't feel any warmth radiating from its metal shell.

Did my crockpot die? Out of the corner of my eye, the green numbers on the microwave blinked 12:00. Of course. A fucking power surge killed the crockpot. *God, I love today.*

I ripped the roll of paper towels off its stand and returned to the living room. I knelt by the puddle, not bothering to wipe the tears welling up my eyes.

Today sucked. First, work. Then, traffic. Now my shitty apartment. It was bad enough that Ryder left me alone while he went on his business trip. I didn't even have Abby anymore to keep me company.

Someone knocked on the door. "Now what?" I mumbled, getting up to peer outside the peephole. My heart skipped a beat when I recognized the spiky black hair and emerald green eyes staring back at me. Ryder returned from his trip! And he was holding a pizza!

I fumbled with the door knob to let him in. "Callie!" he said, wrapping his arms around me. I breathed in his sweet scent - a mixture of cologne and New Herbs soap. Nothing today mattered anymore. He was home.

"When did you get back?" I asked, taking the pizza box and setting it on my coffee table.

He ran a hand through his hair. "This afternoon. I came home earlier to surprise you when I noticed the crockpot wasn't working. I went out to get a pizza, so you wouldn't have to worry about dinner tonight."

I opened the box, my mouth watering at the sight of the pepperoni sitting on top of gooey cheese. "You are so thoughtful! Thank you!"

He gave me another hug. "Of course. Now why don't you grab some plates, and I'll deal with this." He gestured to all the paper towels on the ground.

I pranced into the kitchen to grab a plate out of the cupboard. Tonight, we'd be eating pizza in style. I selected my favorite floral glass plates and returned to the living room. Ryder was hunched over on the floor, mopping up the puddle.

He smiled at me when our eyes met. "Are you hungry?" he asked. "We can worry about the leak after we eat."

We made our plates and sat on the couch. "Let's see what's on Prime," he said, flipping on the TV. We browsed through several movies before settling on an old cartoon we'd watched a million times. "Can't beat a classic," he said as the whimsical theme song played.

I rested my head against his shoulder. "You're the best, you know that?"

He kissed the top of my head. "I try. You sounded so irritated on the phone, I hoped pizza and your favorite show would make your day better."

As we bit into our slices of pizza and laughed at the antics of a talking sponge, I reflected on the events of the day. I was still mad that my boss made me stay late, but...maybe she had saved me from getting into that wreck earlier. And I'm glad my crockpot shorted out. That meant I could enjoy pizza with my favorite guy. Today may have sucked, but that doesn't mean tonight has to.

coded for love

Rose Pulford

"How was the date?" Cici blurted out the second Mei sat down.

Mei glanced at her roommate over the top of her wine glass. It was meant to be a celebratory drink for what Mei had hoped would be a great date.

"Take a guess," she grumbled into her drink.

Cici winced at the sarcasm in her tone. This was her tenth failed first date in three months. Maybe her mother was right, and she was destined to die alone.

"What did this one do?"

Mei glanced around the busy bar. It was like a miniature Times Square piled around the tall high tops. The sounds of laughter and chatter enveloped you into a bubble with the outside world out of reach. The dress code could best be described as 'anything goes.' There were groups of New York housewives sipping wine between groups of businessmen straight from the office for an after-work drink. The clash of business and casual contrasted with the cheesy Irish pub decoration jammed into every corner of O'Neals. It might have felt jarring to others, but to Mei, it reminded her of why she loved living in a city filled with so many different walks of life. She couldn't get enough of it. The other reason she liked O'Neals was that it was only one block away from her apartment and always offered good drinks.

"He tried to have me pay the tab."

"Not great, but surely that isn't the only thing he did wrong."

Mei downed her drink and set the empty wine glass on the bar counter.

"Would you like an itemized list of all the things he did wrong?"

Cici looked like she might take Mei up on her offer, and Mei glared at her. Cici raised her hands in surrender.

"Okay, then, so no Prince Charming. But there are plenty of fish in the sea. When's your next date?"

"I'm done."

"What do you mean?"

"I mean, I'm fully considering becoming a nun."

Cici laughed, drawing the attention of every man in their vicinity. Mei's roommate had no problem finding a new flavor each week. Cici stopped laughing when she could see Mei was serious.

"You can't seriously be thinking of giving up because of a few bad dates? Weren't you the one who said that this would be the year you would end your single streak?"

"A few? I have been on more bad dates these past months than good ones. At this rate, I would be lucky to find someone with whom I even want a second date. It's like the world doesn't want a woman to have it all. Their dream job, apartment, roommate, and man. I'm not even asking for much."

"What are you asking for then?"

"Someone who wants to build a future. Have the happily ever after like they do at the end of the movies."

"But movies are fiction, not reality."

Mei sighed and rested her head in her hands.

"But how could something that so many people talk about experiencing not be real and out there?"

Cici sighed and flagged down one of the bartenders.

"Sounds like we need a bottle."

Mei followed her gaze to one of the most handsome men she'd ever seen, and her breath caught in her chest. He wore the same chic black apron the other bartenders wore, but his clung to a toned body, apparent even under his denim shirt. His robust features were accented by a short beard and man bun, and his green eyes sparkled in the dim light of the bar. He walked over, snapping the towel he was drying his hands on over his shoulder. Mei wasn't generally attracted to this kind of boho chic look, but this man could convert her.

"What can I get you beautiful ladies?"

His bright smile sent goosebumps up Mei's arms. He leaned against the counter, displaying strong forearms with prominent veins that were pure female pornography. The little peak of a tattoo peeking out from where he had rolled up his sleeve was just adding to the tease. Mei caught herself imagining what she would like to do with those forearms and shook herself. She really needed a boyfriend if a random bartender could get her blood boiling like this.

"Bottle of your best Chardonnay and maybe your name," Cici flirted, leaning over the counter.

Mei glanced at his name tag.

"Please ignore my friend, Alex."

Alex chuckled.

"Please, don't," Cici purred.

Alex leaned closer.

"I can definitely get you that bottle, but I think I would much prefer your beautiful friend's number."

Even though Mei assumed this was a tactic he employed often to get bigger tips, she felt her cheeks flush at his brashness. No one had ever been so direct in expressing their interest in her. Genuine or not.

"Just the bottle, please," Mei squeaked out.

Alex shrugged his shoulders with a carefree smile.

He walked away and added, "If you change your mind..."

Mei watched the way his taut muscles moved under his shirt as he retrieved the bottle and uncorked it. It was obvious that he worked out. Mei could feel herself drooling. The slight sting of a snap on her arm snapped her out of her trance-like stare.

"Why did you turn him down?" Cici hissed quietly in her ear, "A gorgeous man literally asked for your number, and you said no?"

"Haven't you been listening?" Mei turned back to her. "I'm becoming a nun. I have given up on dating. I can't do any more of these bad dates, especially with a person I can't vet beforehand."

Cici sighed and leaned back into her bar stool.

"I heard you." Cici pushed her curls back over her ear, "But you can't be serious. To find the right one, you need to get out there."

Mei sighed and rested her head in her hands. Her long dark hair brushed her arms.

"But I'm so tired. It's all too much."

Cici leaned over and patted Mei's back.

"Maybe you're putting too much pressure on yourself. Why not just have fun dating, and not take it seriously?"

"I ... I always pictured one special person out there for me. I'm not like you, Cici."

Cici smiled mischievously, "Fabulously hot and totally unattainable?"

Mei snorted. That was definitely one way to describe Cici and her relationships. In all her time living with Cici in their tiny New York City apartment, she had never seen Cici bring the same guy home twice. She liked changing out her flavors of the week, as she called them, as often as a woman changed her shoes. Mei could never understand how Cici didn't crave that one meaningful connection out of her partnerships, but she was more than happy, so Mei was happy for her then.

"But seriously, it's all too much."

The pair were interrupted by Alex returning with their requested bottle and two clean wine glasses.

"Here you go, ladies."

Under the dim bar lighting, his eyes shone like deep, green pools.

"Now, if you change your mind about that number, please feel free to call me over."

Mei straightened in her seat, her cheeks turning pink. Alex smiled, his eyes pinning Mei to her seat. Her pulse quickened under the intensity of his gaze. Mei could feel an elbow dig into her side. Cici was smirking over her glass.

"Are you sure about that? He does look pretty good. Plus, he pours a good glass of wine."

Mei blushed and Alex spared her from answering by walking across the bar to attend to another customer.

"I prefer my men more nerdy. Someone who would at least understand a little of what I'm talking about with my work and doesn't get that glazed over look when I say things like coding and neural networks."

Mei couldn't help giggling over Cici perfectly rearranging her face into a blank expression with a far off distant look. Mei shoved her in the arm, which snapped Cici into joining her in a fit of giggles. When their laughter finally died down, they both turned back to their drinks.

"Still," Cici said, "I would climb that man like a tree."

Mei shook her head. Her friend was something else.

"But seriously, what's next?" Cici asked.

"No idea."

The two women fell into a comfortable silence while sipping their wine. Mei appreciated that Cici didn't immediately try to placate her or call her desire for long term commitment delusional. The chatter from all the patrons filled the space between them. Finally, Cici broke the silence.

"You're an AI developer, right?"

Mei paused, wine halfway to her mouth.

"Yeah. What does that have to do with anything?"

Cici kicked back the rest of her glass of wine, "Why don't you create some sort of thingy that will find your Mr. Right?"

Mei didn't say anything, but let Cici's words sink in.

"You're a genius when it comes to creating these things, so why not have it do the work of narrowing down the possible men straight to the one? Take the work off of you to guess if this guy is the one."

Mei snorted, dismissing Cici's crazy idea. The rest of the evening was spent polishing off the bottle of wine, and bitching some more about the tragedy of being a modern woman in New York. At the end of their bottle, they walked arm in arm for the one-block journey home and passed out on their living room couches.

The next morning when Mei woke up with the world's biggest hangover, she couldn't stop thinking about what Cici had said. What if she could create an AI match-making system? One that would be able to figure out if the people meeting up were perfect for each other or not. It could account for compatibility, attractiveness, values, and even verify identity. She wouldn't have to sit through all those awful dates. The system could spit out the perfect man. Mei pulled out her laptop and immediately began working on building out the AI that was going to set her up with Mr. Perfect. It might be the craziest, best idea Cici has ever had.

———————

Mei's heart pounded in her chest – it was five months later and she was actually executing Cici's absurd idea. On a normal day, product launches thrilled her. Taking a vision and bringing it to life was entirely why she got into her field. However, creating an AI for her own personal mission of finding Mr. Right was the highlight of her career thus far.

"How's the matchmaking going? Find true love yet?"

Mei looked up from the lines of code to see Cici drop her gym bag on the living room floor. Mei tried not to roll her eyes at Cici's teasing. This wasn't the first time that she had used that line this week alone.

"Reviewing the last line of code."

Cici stared back at her, happily sipping her expensive smoothie, which she always treated herself to whenever she taught an especially good fitness class. Cici was an enthusiastic Pilates teacher.

"Stop staring at me like that." Mei lifted her laptop from her lap and unfolded her legs from under her.

"I can't help it! You're actually going through with this. Building an entire AI system to try to find yourself true love."

This time Mei couldn't help it. She rolled her eyes, and reached for the half empty wine glass she left on the coffee table last night.

"Well, not all of us are happy with endless amounts of one-night stands. Besides, it was your idea in the first place."

Cici pinched the bridge of her nose. "I was joking."

"Well, I'm not. Fabio is going to find my soulmate. He's programmed with advice from the top matchmakers and dating coaches. From the practical to the astrological. I inputted all my preferences and parameters. He has all he needs to find a match."

Cici raised an eyebrow. "You named the system Fabio? Like the cover model on all those romance books?"

Mei could feel her cheeks heating.

"It seemed fitting."

Cici scoffed. Her curls bounced as she crossed the room to stand directly in front of Mei, "I'm sure. Promise me that you won't marry the first guy Fabio puts before you."

Mei shrugged with her wine glass in her hand, "Why not? He has all the parameters. I connected him to all the top dating apps. I gave him my basic profile to use and scour the options with. Fabio is going to be my ultimate matchmaker."

"I don't think so."

"Why not?"

"Maybe because love is a lot more complicated than a line of coding, Mei."

"How would you know?"

"I may choose to be the Queen of One Night Stands, but that doesn't mean I don't know about love or haven't toyed with it before."

A small frown tugged at the corner of Cici's mouth.

"Trust me," Cici said, "Love has a way of coming from some of the most unexpected places, and won't often be what you expect. You can't pair people together just based on their lifestyles and physical attraction. It doesn't work like that."

Mei stared down at her laptop letting Cici's words sink in. She trusted Cici in a lot of things, but she wasn't sure that she could with this. Cici changed out guys like one changes out accessories, and it never bothered her that not one ever seemed to come back around. Actually, Cici seemed to revel in needing no one else except herself. But Mei wasn't like that.

Mei thought back to the many nights she had come home from work to an empty apartment just to eat dinner by herself in front of the TV. She hated those nights the most, because once she turned off the TV. The silence would creep from the edges of the apartment and threaten to drown her. Even with the constant background music of ambulances and traffic, it wasn't enough to keep the loneliness away. She didn't think this was what her life was going to be like in thirties.

Mei had always thought that by now she would have the home with white picket fence, the two point five kids, and a husband who was there for her in the good times and the bad. Although her career had taken off, her love life was stalled.

Mei was proud to be considered one of the top leading AI architects in the country with businesses banging on her door begging her to work with them. She got to pick which projects she got to work on, and had control over which of her co-workers she wanted working with her. But Mei still lived in the same tiny apartment with the same roommate since she'd graduated from college with. Far from what she'd pictured.

"I'm just tired of being alone. I want it all, Cici, and I haven't been able to so far. That's why I have to believe in the system I designed."

Cici sighed and collapsed on the couch next to her.

"Ok. Walk me through what parameters you gave this Fabio for finding your perfect match. I'm guessing you asked for nerdy, but socially clueless?"

Mei shoved her elbow into Cici's ribs, eliciting a laugh.

"Yes and no. I did put in someone smart, nerdy, refined, and successful—someone sweet and charming, like a combo of Chris Evans and Benedict Cumberbatch."

"Basically, Prince Charming riding on a white horse."

Mei rolled her eyes, "I'm being serious here."

Cici stared at Mei for a while longer before sighing. She stood and collected her gym bag from the floor, "Don't be sad when it doesn't work out, ok?"

Cici turned on her heel before walking off to her room, leaving Mei alone with her laptop.

"It's going to work!" Mei shouted after her.

When there was no answer, Mei rolled her eyes and took another sip from her wine glass. This was going to work. She knew it. She was going to prove Cici wrong.

With that thought, Mei set her wine glass back down on the coffee table. She wrapped her manicured hands around her laptop, pulling it closer, took a deep breath and hit enter. She watched lines of codes morph and change to a collage of colors as profiles whizzed across her screen, names and likes indistinguishable from the next.

———

Mei looked over her outfit in the bathroom mirror of O' Neal's. She could hear the clanking of dishes and shouts for orders on the other side of the wall from the kitchen. Fabio had done his job and found her a match. Now, Mr. Right should be sitting at the bar waiting for her. Mei tried to smooth some invisible wrinkles in her dress. Her palms felt sweaty, and she took a deep breath.

This was it. She was going to get everything that she wanted. She couldn't decide whether to scream for joy or collapse into a puddle. Cici hadn't helped her nerves by laughing at the profile when she shared it with her.

Mei had committed to memory all that she knew about Bryce Adams. He was a biology professor at NYU, loved a good night in, but was also open to exploring new places. When she saw his photo, Mei thought he was good looking enough in his bowtie and khakis. Not drop your panties good looking, but there was nothing wrong with that. It was what was inside that counted.

Looking over Mei's shoulder back in their apartment, Cici had offered her unsolicited opinion. "I hate to burst your bubble, but he looks extremely boring."

"What do you mean?" Mei had asked.

"His profile reads like the bio of Professor Plum."

Mei had rolled her eyes and stomped away from the laughing Cici.

Cici could laugh all she wanted, but Mei was going to trust the AI she built. She wasn't going to spend another minute sitting around by herself and waiting. If Fabio said this guy was her perfect match, she was going to believe it.

With a deep breath, she grabbed her clutch off the counter and went back out into the bar. The sound of laughter and talking poured over her along with the familiar soft soundtrack of O'Neal's.

Mei slid into one of the open bar stools and began scanning the Saturday night crowd for her date.

"Hey, stranger."

Mei turned to see the bartender, Alex. Looking as handsome as she remembered, he still wore his casual smirk. His shirt pulled tight against his forearms. Mei would never admit that he had starred in a few fantasies of hers, but she called on her self restraint. She was a woman on a mission, and no cute bartender was going to distract her from it. Mei could feel her cheeks heat as she greeted him back.

"It's been a while since I last saw you," he said, leaning closer, "Something been keeping you away?"

"Not really."

"Like what?"

"You wouldn't understand."

Alex's smile widened, "Try me."

It was the kind of smile that you saw in toothpaste ads. So open and honest. It made Mei want to tell him everything. Mei shrugged, ignoring her pounding heart.

"Well, –"

"Hi. Are you Mei?" a new voice cut her off.

This was it. Mei took a deep breath and turned around. She froze.

Bryce, her date, was not what she had pictured at all. He still had on the cute frames from his profile photo, but he sported an oversized navy suit jacket over a pink polo and khakis. Mei tried not to frown.

This was not how she imagined her future love would look like. Mei tried to shrug off her first impression. She shouldn't think like that. Love was blind, after all. So what if he had a bad fashion sense? Fabio had specifically picked out this man from the hundreds of profiles out there based on her specific requirements, so he was bound to be perfect for her.

"Hi. Bryce, right?"

Bryce nodded and pulled up the seat next to her at the bar. The bar stool screeched against the floor, cutting through the sounds of the busy Saturday night crowd. Mei winced at the sound and glanced back to Alex, who looked amused.

Mei couldn't help but trace her eyes over his muscular chest. Now, that is how a man can look attractive without even trying. She might have been imagining it, but did Alex puff his chest out a little more? Too bad he was the bartender and not her date.

"What can I get you?" Alex asked.

Bryce adjusted his glasses and fiddled with the bar napkin before him.

"Do you have a mocktail I could order? I'm not really much of a drinker."

"Why didn't you say so?" Mei asked. "If I'd known, I would have suggested another place," Mei said.

"It's ok. I wanted to see what one of your favorite places was."

Mei smiled at the sweet gesture.

"So, like a Shirley Temple or a Roy Rogers?" Alex interrupted him.

"I have no idea what a Roy Rogers is, so the Shirley Temple

please."

While Bryce adjusted his glasses, Mei could feel the heat of Alex's stare on the side of her face. She allowed herself a quick glance at him and could hear the unspoken question in his gaze. *That is your type?*

She cleared her throat.

"Wine for me, please, Alex."

Alex's eyes lit up with a smile, and Mei felt the mortification wash over in waves as she realized she had called the bartender by his name. She snapped back to her date, who seemed to not notice anything about their little exchange. From the corner of her eye, Mei could see Alex's eyes still fixed on her. His movements of opening bottles and pouring into each glass were done so effortlessly. He did it all without looking.

Mei squirmed under the spotlight of his attention, and pinched her palm to bring herself back to the present. She wasn't a heroine in one of her novels as Cici loved to point out. She was on a date with her perfect match. She needed to pay attention to him, not the bartender, who was probably working on his tip. Mei spun around in her chair until she was face to face with Bryce once again. She pasted on her most perfect smile.

"Tell me about yourself. Any hobbies?" Mei asked.

Just like that, the date with Bryce was up and running. If you could call it that. By the end of her first glass of wine, Mei had never been so bored in her life. Near the end of her second drink, she was close to stabbing her hand with her fork in order to stay awake.

"My friends and I have a trip planned out to the Appalachian Trail next fall to collect further evidence of BigFoot since that has been where the latest sightings have been. We're going to prove that BigFoot exists just like that New Guinea big eared bat that everyone thought was extinct."

Mei nodded while sipping her drink. She discreetly looked at her watch.

"Don't you agree?"

Mei snapped herself to attention.

"I guess –"

"Exactly! I knew you would understand."

Bryce kept his monologue going without looking at Mei, and she tried to hold back her sigh. The entire evening had been like this and she wasn't sure how much longer she could take. On paper, she and Bryce were a perfect match, but this date could only be described as another disaster. How did Fabio fail so badly? Its entire job was to find her perfect soulmate and it had clearly failed.

Bryce took a sip from his drink and Mei was grateful for a break from the onslaught of words.

Was this person really meant to be the one for her?

Mei sighed into her wine glass and tried to sip at the empty glass. Forever after was starting to look a whole lot more depressing if this was what she had to look forward to. Mei shook the thought from her head. Maybe it was first-date jitters. Maybe it wouldn't be so bad once he got used to her. Mei forced her eyes to look forward at Bryce and hum her response when appropriate.

Bryce was covering the great intricacies of Charles Dickens when Mei couldn't help but let her gaze drift to the walking Michelangelo named Alex. As if he could sense her gaze on him, Alex's eyes met hers. She could feel her palms become sweaty. Mei shifted in her seat at the sheer intensity of his gaze. Bryce's droning voice faded from her mind. Her full attention was captured by the eyes that had longed to follow her.

Alex's eyes darkened the longer she held his gaze. A smirk played on his lips. Goosebumps crept up her bare arms. Her full focus was encompassed by the single man she didn't think she could ever want.

Alex started crossing the bar back towards them. Mei shifted in her bar stool, and her heart skipped a beat. What was he doing?

Bryce rambled on, oblivious. He gestured enthusiastically with his arms. He clearly had no idea of the stares Mei and Alex were sharing.

There was a small voice screaming in the back of her mind that she should wave him off, but no words fell from her lips. Her fingers bunched the fabric of her dress, while she fought the urge to get up. It was like her body was warring with her mind.

"Why don't you let the lady get a word in?"

Bryce jumped at Alex's voice. His hand knocked into the cocktail glass, and Mei braced herself for the red liquid splashing towards her. *Oh no. Please don't.* She reached out her hands to try to catch it, but it was already too late. Red spilled all over Mei's lap.

The sound of glass shattering broke the warm frenzied air of the bar as patrons turned to stare. Mei froze as the liquid seeped into her clothes. She looked up at Bryce, who was quiet and growing pale. Great. Another thing has gone wrong tonight. Mei scrambled to get off the stool.

"Give me a minute."

She didn't wait for Bryce to reply before crossing the busy bar to the bathrooms. When she finally was able to click the bathroom door into place, she stared at the giant stain on her favorite dress. Mei closed her eyes against the tears. What was wrong with her? Fabio had done what she'd asked and picked a guy that fit all her requirements, but here she was, barely surviving another bad first date. The worst part was that it wasn't even over yet.

She was supposed to be the top AI architect in the world and she had failed. In fact, Mei wanted nothing to do with Byrce. There was just no way that he could be her forever. Mei let out a humorless laugh. She had done everything right. She had built the perfect combination of machine learning and neural network to sort out the ideal match yet here she was, miserable again. Mei dragged herself to the sink. She grabbed some paper towels to begin scrubbing at the mess, while her mind reeled with questions. What went wrong?

With each new question, her hands scrubbed harder at the stain. Memories began flooding her head. The numerous weddings she had attended without a date. The interrogations from her family about when she was going to settle down. Every memory like a small dagger drawing itself deeper and deeper into her. Mei kept rubbing and rubbing until the towels fell apart in her hands. Mei sighed and set her hands against the sink.

Glancing at the mirror, she took in her appearance. A red flush traveled down to her chest, where she could see each stuttering breath she took. She had never seen herself like this before. Mei straightened her dress and fixed her hair. She needed to clear her head and salvage this date. She wasn't going to let her happily ever after slip through her fingers. Standing tall, with her shoulders back and chin lifted, Mei walked back out across the bar. Bryce's stool was empty.

Mei tried to look for him, but it was hard to see past all the people milling around the bar. Maybe he got up to get something.

"Your date paid for your drinks and ran out of here," Alex's smooth voice called out to her.

Mei could feel her shoulders slump, and the stinging of tears back in her eyes. How did it go so wrong? Bryce had everything that she was looking for. Mei slid back into her bar stool.

"Can I have a glass of water?"

Alex nodded, and Mei rested her head down on her arms. The sound of laughter from the other patrons was sandpaper against her nerves. She looked up when she felt something cold touch her arm and found herself looking into Alex's concerned face, who now held two glasses—one clearly with water and the other filled with bright orange and red. He set them both down in front of her.

"I didn't order this," Mei said, trying to slide the colorful glass back to him.

Alex only smiled and pushed the glass back towards her. His growing smile revealed a small dimple peeking out from the corner of his cheek.

"It looked like you could use it."

Mei looked back down at the glass. She must have really looked pathetic if the bartender was trying to cheer her up during his peak busy hours. She looked at the glass and played with the bar napkin under it.

"Thank you, but that wasn't necessary."

He shrugged, and reached under the counter to pull out a glass, which he absently began wiping down with the cloth from his apron. Mei relaxed when she realized that he wasn't going to push her.

She examined the cocktail in front of her. Wine had been her drink of choice tonight, but she did love a good cocktail. Curious, Mei picked up the bright drink and took a tentative sip. Bright sweet notes of fruit and acidic citrus danced on her tongue. This was exactly the kind of cocktail she liked to order when she went out for drinks. Mei looked up at Alex, who was still absently wiping down his glass.

"How did you...?"

He let out a cheeky grin, and his dimple made another appearance. Mei fought her own smile.

"It's my talent," Alex shrugged.

"A good talent to have."

Mei took another sip of her cocktail, enjoying the rush of flavours on her tongue, followed by the sting of alcohol at the end.

"Want to talk about it?"

Mei choked on her drink before returning it to the counter.

"Not really."

Mei began fidgeting with the cocktail napkin and Alex leaned against the countertop, their arms nearly touching.

"If I take a guess, could you tell me if I'm hot or cold?"

Mei nodded, though she was pretty sure everyone in the bar knew what happened.

"Was he an alien disguised as a human recounting all of his findings on the human species?"

Mei snorted. She took a sip of her water, feeling a touch light-headed.

"I wish that were true. Then my night might have actually been interesting."

Alex tapped his chin like he was thinking.

"Was it the presentation of his dissertation on the failing of the public school systems?"

Mei allowed a small smile, though the corners of it didn't quite reach her eyes.

"It's ok. You can say what it was. A bad first date. One in a long series of many that I've been having lately."

Mei didn't meet Alex's eyes. She chose instead to look around the bar at all the other customers. Everywhere she looked, happy couples and groups of friends huddled together, laughing and smiling. She was the only one alone.

She felt a warm rough hand on top of hers. Mei turned back to Alex.

"It happens. It's not the end of the world."

Mei sighed.

"It's not that."

"What is it then?" Alex asked.

"I couldn't feel anything."

She decided to be a little truthful. It wasn't like Alex really cared about what was going on. Mei began playing with the cocktail napkin again. Her eyes rested on the glass in front of her.

"What do you mean?"

Mei sighed. She looked up at the emerald pools of Alex's eyes boring straight through to her soul. The words tumbled out of her before she could stop them.

"He was supposed to be the love of my life, and I didn't feel anything."

Mei could feel a blush painting her cheeks as she realized what she said.

"Why did you think that?" he asked with genuine curiosity.

Mei sighed, debating whether or not to spill everything to a stranger. In a city like New York, filled with thousands of people, they would probably never run into each other again anyway. Mei leaned back into her bar stool, preparing her heart.

"It was what Fabio told me."

"Who's Fabio?"

"Fabio is -"

A ding rang out from her purse. Pausing, Mei grabbed her phone and opened it to see one new notification

Fabio has found a match!

Mei felt as if she'd been dunked into cold water. She looked up at Alex, his curious gaze trying to read her phone screen from his position across the bar top. What was she doing? She should be out there arranging a date with her next perfect match, not sitting here chatting up a man who was so far from what she was looking for it wasn't even funny. Even if Alex was sweet. And witty. And genuine.

"Fabio is no one."

Mei closed her phone and began collecting her purse. She needed to get out of there.

"I have to go. How much do I owe you for the drink?"

He shook his head.

"On the house."

Mei hesitated before leaving. She wasn't really sure when or how she got back to her apartment until her back leaned against her door.

"What's the matter with you?" asked Cici as Mei burst through the apartment door. She held in her hands a pint of ice cream.

Without a second thought, Mei dropped her purse to the ground and made a beeline right for the ice cream. She snatched it out of Cici's hands.

"Give me that. Right now, I need it more than you."

Mei continued into the kitchen, opening drawers and trying to find a spoon.

"Want to clue me in as to why you stole my ice cream?"

Mei grunted as she found what she was looking for. Ignoring Cici, she grabbed a big spoonful of ice cream.

"That's not an answer."

Mei shoved the spoonful in her mouth and grimaced at a wave of brain freeze. When the pain subsided , Mei looked to Cici, who was now blocking the entrance to the kitchen, hands on her hips. She wasn't going to let this go. Mei sighed and dropped the spoon back into the container before passing it back to Cici. With a deep breath, she recounted everything that had happened, from the surprising appearance of Bryce to the fatal wine spill to the pity drink from the bartender.

"Maybe it's a sign."

Mei snorted, "Sign for what? I'm destined to die alone with my collection of romance novels."

Cici shrugged her shoulders, "Maybe Mr. Right is standing right in front of you, and no AI system can help you find it."

Mei rolled her eyes, "What, Alex? He was being nice and playing his part as the friendly bartender."

"I don't know. I have a sense about these things, and something tells me that there's something more going on there."

Mei couldn't deny that. She had clearly been distracted by his looks tonight and he wasn't bad to talk to. But she was sure there was nothing more.

"What are you going to do about the other match that Fabio found for you?"

Mei stole another bite of ice cream from Cici. Cici pulled back, but didn't take her gaze off of Mei.

"I think I'm going on another date with the guy Fabio found. I mean, maybe the first one was just a fluke. All systems have a few bugs and kinks to work out after the launch."

Cici raised an eyebrow, "Are you sure about this?"

Mei shrugged and darted her spoon forward to steal another bite of ice cream. Cici dodged and slapped her hand away.

Another date. Another dress.

Mei stood outside of O'Neals, frozen in place. The shake in her hands was getting worse by the minute. It was another busy Saturday night, with the bar packed full.. The music and boisterous laughter spilled out onto the sidewalk. She shouldn't have come back here.

Cici had convinced her that going back to the same place was a good idea to not only replace the bad memories but also take advantage of O'Neals' casual environment, which Cici said was perfect for getting to know someone. Also, Cici said that she wasn't giving up their favorite bar just because of a bad date. Mei couldn't argue with her on that point. After another couple of nights sitting at home alone after work, Mei agreed with Cici to get back on the horse. Mei was determined to not be alone any longer. Plus, she may not have been great at relationships but she could build a damn good AI system. The last time had to just have been a fluke. A pure miscalculation, she had told herself. This time it was going to be it.

However, as she walked through the heavy wooden doors, she froze. It wasn't the memories of her bad date that held her in place. Her breath quickened at the thought of a particular man's attention which she didn't escape that night. His eyes and voice were the things that stuck with her the most, even when she tried so hard to forget them. Mei prayed he wasn't working tonight. She needed to focus on her date and not get distracted by Alex.

For a brief moment, Mei wondered if it would be too late to cancel her date with her newest match, Jordan Kieser. He was a self-made entrepreneur, who owned a finance firm. In his profile picture, he had looked clean cut and with a decent sense of fashion compared to her last match. A more promising start to finding love already. Using one of the deep breath techniques that Cici had taught her, Mei forced one foot in front of the other.

She pushed past the jumbled bodies in the bar until she found an empty stool in a secluded corner. It was far enough away from the rowdy crowds of a Saturday night that one could actually hear someone else speak but still observe all the activities around them. Mei took another practiced breath. She looked down to see that her hands were still shaking. Maybe a drink would help. Mei signaled to the bartenders, who were busy flying from one order to the next.

"You're back," a familiar voice called out.

Mei's brown eyes locked onto Alex's emerald ones. Mei gulped.

Of course, Alex was working tonight.

Alex leaned his elbows against the bar top and leaned in close. His eyes trailing over every inch of her that he could see. Mei couldn't help shivering. His gaze felt as intimate as a physical touch.

"Did you get all dressed up just for me?"

Mei could feel the blush staining her cheeks at Alex's smile. She didn't think she'd ever seen a sexier smile.

"N-no," she choked out, "I'm meeting my date here."

Alex leaned back, "The mysterious Fabio, I take it?"

She couldn't believe he remembered their last conversation. It had been over a week. "Kind of."

Alex raised an eyebrow but didn't push, "What can I get the beautiful lady, then, while she awaits this missing date?"

Mei flushed, thinking about how much she drank the last time she was here. She didn't want to repeat that, but a little something to take the edge off wouldn't hurt. "Can I get that cocktail drink that you made me the last time? I don't know the name of it, but it was very good."

Alex nodded and began moving around the bar with ease. Mei watched as his practiced hands moved in such a way that only came with experience and time. Before long, she had a perfect recreation of the bright orange and red drink. As she reached out to take the glass, she felt her hand encased in warmth. Mei looked up shocked to see Alex staring deeply into her eyes while holding her hand in his.

"If you were my date, I would never keep you waiting."

Mei gasped. *This is a game to him*, she tried to remind herself, but somewhere in her gut she knew that the intensity in his eyes was real. After an eternity had passed, Alex let her hand go. Mei released the breath she'd been holding, , but didn't look away. Not even as her hand slipped around the cold glass set before her. Mei took a sip. She closed her eyes as the bright sweet notes of fruit and acidic citrus filled her mouth.

"Just as good?"

Mei nodded. , and Alex turned his attention to another patron flagging him down. Mei forced herself to take a calming breath and adjusted the skirt of her dress. She checked her phone to see no new messages. It was still early but she had expected to hear from her date at least confirming the time and location for tonight.

Mei looked around the bar, searching for someone resembling the profile of her latest match. However, in the sea of faces, she didn't recognize a single one. Mei sighed and sipped at her drink. It was all a waiting game now.

As her glass turned into melted cubes of ice, Mei felt sweat beading at the back of her neck. Patrons had come and gone. The music over the speakers had changed from some pop hit to something more sultry and slow. Mei stared helplessly at her phone. No new messages. She didn't know whether to scream or cry. How could this be happening again? Feeling a sudden urge to flee, Mei's shaky hands grabbed her purse, and she began searching for her wallet. A hand rested on her shoulder, startling her, and Mei turned to see the smiling face of Alex holding a cocktail and beer in one hand. Gone was the usual towel tucked into his belt. A few strands of hair had escaped his man bun, making him look deliciously disheveled

"Sorry for running late. I hope it's ok that I grabbed you another drink."

Mei opened and closed her mouth, not sure how to reply. Alex set the glasses down on the bar before pulling out the stool next to her. With each movement, he brushed against her in some way. Goosebumps rising from each touch. Mei leaned in to whisper, "What are you doing?"

"Playing the part of Prince Charming. I'm the best they could find in a pinch."

The scent of his cologne was intoxicating. Was this really happening? Alex leaned back in his chair, tipping his beer back.

"What about your work?"

"The other bartenders can handle it. This is more important. My mom taught me to never let a pretty woman sit by herself unless she wants to."

Mei tried to draw a breath into her tight chest. She turned back to the cocktail he'd brought her and took a sip.

"By the way, Fabio is an idiot."

"Fabio isn't an idiot."

"Of course, he is. No sane guy would have left you here on your own."

"If you call Fabio an idiot, you might as well be calling me one too."

Alex blinked, obviously confused.

Mei chuckled, "Since I built him."

"You built him?"

Mei took another drink.

"Yep. Fabio is the artificial intelligence algorithm I developed to find my soulmate."

"You're saying that you built a program to find a date?"

Mei lowered her gaze, self conscious. It did sound insane.

"That's so cool. How did you do that?"

Mei's eyes snapped back up to Alex's in shock. His wide eyes and smile showed genuine interest. She couldn't believe it.

She cleared her throat, "Um I used data from various dating apps and different theories from highly regarded matchmakers. I combined each of them to find what should be my perfect match."

Alex sipped his drink, thinking, his eyebrows drawn together in concentration.

"Can you give me an example of some of the parameters that you used?"

Mei smiled before launching into a technical breakdown of everything she did. How she had pulled the data from several dating apps, and then cross-referenced with social media to make sure that they weren't seeing anyone else. How she had built data scraping into the system to extract the relevant information from each profile then used that information with the latest dating psychology to either eliminate the profile or use it to create her viable dating pool.

Alex's eyes shone with interest. He nodded in all the right places, allowing Mei to continue talking. Not once did he get that glazed over look that so many guys did when she talked about her work.

"Then, Fabio is more of a Reactive AI than a Theory of Mind AI system?" Alex asked.

"Basically," Mei nodded before sighing into her drink, "But as you can see, that clearly hasn't been working."

"Sadly, your pool is limited since not everyone is on dating apps."

"What do you mean? Of course, everyone is on dating apps."

"I'm not."

Mei blinked. *Was he serious?* He was gorgeous. Hundreds of girls would message him. He would have to bat them off like flies.

"How can you not be?"

Alex chuckled.

Both of them went quiet, allowing the chatter of the bar to fill the space between them.

"I don't think love is something that you can code for or find behind a screen."

Mei's eyebrows pinched together, "What do you mean?"

Alex took a sip of his beer, "Anyone can have the qualities you're looking for, but love is something that deals with your heart. It doesn't involve being logical. It's nice when it does, but that isn't always the case."

Mei rested her head against her hand and studied Alex, turning over his words in her head.

"Logic is the basis of everything."

Alex laughed out loud. The rich, deep tones enveloped Mei. She didn't mind him laughing at her. In fact, she wanted more of that.

"Humans are not always rational beings. Especially when it comes to matters of the heart."

"Not true." She insisted.

"Name one romance movie where the leads get together based solely on logic alone."

Mei thought back to her piles of romance books at home. How each story was filled with the challenges, doubts, and obstacles of the real world before their feelings took over and the main characters decided that they couldn't live without each other. Mei met his gaze, only inches from her. Maybe he had a point.

"How do you know so much about romances?"

"I have two little sisters. They were obsessed with romance and fairy tales from a young age."

"That makes you an expert?"

He laughed and leaned back.

"Osmosis by association."

Her eyebrows lifted at the scientific reference and Alex chuckled.

"I used to work in the tech industry before I got tired of all the corporate rules. Then I partnered with one of my chef friends and we opened this place together."

"Wait, so you run this place?"

"Yep. I like helping the bartenders when I'm free so I can see how everything is working on the floor. It's good to be hands-on."

Mei blinked her eyes, trying to imagine this man in front of her ever being like one of the tech bros that she works with. She couldn't picture it with his long blonde hair tied up in a man bun, perfectly trimmed facial hair, and tattoos all over his arms.

"I know, hard to believe, right? It was a relief when I made the transition."

Silence fell between them again, but this time it didn't feel forced or awkward.

"But seriously. According to your logic, I wouldn't be sitting here. I shouldn't have even tried to hit on you that first time that we met. I can't help thinking what a shame that would have been."

Alex spun his beer bottle in his hand, and continued, "I'm going to be honest with you. I feel a pull towards you that I have never felt towards another woman. It's kind of why I haven't been able to keep my eyes off of you since that first night that we met. And that feeling tells me that we might just work despite what your Fabio may say."

Mei stared into his eyes. The weight of each of his words pulled her deeper into his gaze. Her skin buzzed with electricity. She had never felt like this before. Not with any of her exes or her supposed matches. Only with Alex.

"But you don't know anything about me. Not really."

"I can see your soul in your eyes and your heart on your sleeve. Right now, that's enough reason for me."

Alex trailed his hand into her hair. His calloused fingers weaved through the escaped tendrils that trailed along her neck. Mei couldn't help the little moan that came out of her in response. Her eyes closed at the sensation of his skin touching hers.

A ding jolted her out of Alex's hold.

A new match! From Fabio.

Mei's attention was torn from his touch to the phone on the counter.

"What are you going to do?"

Mei felt pulled between logic and passion. Should she open Fabio and see what new match was on the horizon, or should she enjoy the man in front of her? Mei took a steadying breath.

"Mei, will you go on a date with me?"

Mei closed the app and placed her phone face down on the bar top. She met Alex's eyes and returned his smile.

the measure

David Hansen

It's not that I'm not over her
It's been five years, six this summer.
It's just that she showed me so clearly
What it was like to be an unmasked, free flowing me.

And whether she knew it or not,
She loved me.
Loved me like no one had before or since.
Because what else is total freedom when with her,
If not love?

And it's not that I'm not over her,
It's that the self understanding she gifted me
Is the measure for every connection since.
Not comparing others to her,
But to their influence on my sense of expandability.

How could you not think fondly of such a benefactor?
How could you not miss the possibility of discovery?
How could you not carry a gratitude unending?
Frankly, I don't want those answers.

Because, it was the most wonderful
And the most difficult thing, being with her.
That I felt so completely for her? Beautiful.
But her feelings faded? ... Fuck.

Maybe I was unable to give her
the same gift she gave me.
Or maybe she was unable to receive it,
Either way, we didn't work for her.

It's not that I'm not over her,
It's been five years, six this summer.
It's that the streams of our lives,
Ran together for a time, exquisitely.
And my soul can never forget.

joe

Amanda Kennedy

The group of teenagers loitered around the front of the hardware store under a streetlight swarmed by moths. Aside from the moth frenzy, the night was still. Traffic in the small town had died down to nothing and it had been almost an hour since even one car had driven by. The kids, ranging in age from fourteen to nineteen, were bored.

"Hey, Cayla," said Mark, pulling his cigarette from his lips to blow a smoke ring. "I bet you can't touch your elbows behind your back."

To the delight of the boys, Cayla took the bet. Her breasts pushed forward, straining against her white t-shirt. Laughter broke and she joined them; clueless or indulgent was anyone's guess.

"You guys! You guys! What? Why are you laughing?" She tried once more then dropped her arms to her sides. "Okay, I give up. I can't do it. What's so funny? Mark, stop laughing!"

Seated on the concrete steps, Lisa was not laughing. She was tired of answering Joe's whispered inquiries of *what's wrong*, with curt replies of *nothing*, and subtly moving away from him while he worked just as hard to close the gap between them. She knew this would go on all night if she stayed. So, even though it was only eleven o'clock, plenty of time for something to happen, she stood up and declared that she was tired and going home.

"I'll walk you home," said Joe, standing up, too.

Lisa crossed her arms over her chest. "No, thanks. I'm ok. Good-night, guys." She pretended not to notice Joe lean in for a kiss as she turned and walked away.

Home was only a ten-minute walk through the quiet, small town streets. Black skies full of stars yawned wide overhead. If she lived in a city, walking home alone at this time of night might have been unwise, but it was safe here. Criminal activity in this small town was limited to vandalism (by the drunken under eighteen crowd), and bar fights (by the drunken over eighteen crowd).

With the stress of how to handle her impending break-up weighing heavy on her, it was a great relief to be alone after fielding unwanted attention from Joe all night. The empty streets offered themselves to her and she walked right up the middle. Having so much unobstructed space, she lifted her eyes to the sky and challenged herself to see how far she could walk without looking down. She exhaled into the stars above. She could never get more than a dozen steps or so. Fear of the unknown got to her.

Approaching her house, it was no surprise to Lisa that the lights were out. Her mom and stepdad turned in early each night. She went through the gate to the backyard and rounded the corner of the small house. A small sound made her stop to listen. Had the night not been so silent, she might not have heard the soft, high pitched squeaking coming from the other corner of the back of the house. Her stepdad had built a small shed in the tight space between the house and the fence, and Lisa hurried over, recognizing the sound as she got closer..

Silently, she took hold of the shed's door handle and pulled it open against the spring. It was dark inside, but the full moon gave enough light for her to see her cat, Kiwi, and six brand new, just licked clean kittens in a cardboard box. Lisa slowly knelt in the doorway to inspect the adorably ugly kittens nursing and mewing at their mother's soft pink belly.

"Kiwi..." Lisa half mouthed, half breathed. She'd known her cat was expecting soon, but was nonetheless enraptured with their arrival. Kiwi wore the exhausted look of all mothers in the minutes after labor. She made the slightest effort to lift her calico head from the ground and opened her eyes just enough to register who was there. She acknowledged her human with a scratchy mew, put her head back down, and closed her eyes. Lisa knew not to betray Kiwi's trust by coming any closer.

Joy bubbled up inside of her and spilled into the empty night, wasted. She craved someone to share it with. Someone whom she could look over at and see her same wonder reflected back to her. Someone who recognized the beauty in these blind, mewing, helpless little creatures. Brand new life that could be contained in the palm of your hand.

The first person who came to mind was Joe.

Joe was a gentle soul. He wrote poetry in elegant calligraphy, crafted love letters in Polaroid pictures, and smiled from his deep brown eyes. His voice was soft, his words were kind, and his heart was generous. And tonight, his meek spirit, and willingness to go along with whatever anyone wanted, which had begun to annoy her, were exactly what she wanted.

Lisa softly closed the shed door, careful not to disturb Kiwi, and tiptoed away. Once she was across the yard and through the gate, she took off running. The excitement of showing the kittens to Joe turned her into a natural runner for all of the five minutes it took to get there. As she was about to round the corner, it occurred to her that they might not still be where she left them, which only multiplied her happiness that they were.

"Yo! Look who's back!"

"Hey, Lisa, do you want a job planting tulips? Get it? *Two Lips*."

Raucous laughter followed. She ignored them and ran straight to Joe. She was self aware enough to feel guilty at the way his eyes lit up when he saw her coming for him. It broke her heart a little. She took his hand; the hand she'd been pulling away from all night, and said,

"Come on. I want to show you something."

Mark laughed, "I want to see, too!"

But they were already running away, back to Lisa's house. Joe was laughing his infectious hearty chuckle and asking, "What is it? What are you showing me?" He had a beautiful laugh. More beautiful than any boy's laugh she'd ever heard or would ever hear again.

"You'll see." She looked back at him and they shared an uncomplicated smile. Full of love. Not the fully developed, hard earned romantic love of adults, but the pure love of human connection, the love of exhilaration, the innocent love of holding hands and running down an empty street at night.

He kept laughing and allowed himself to be pulled along. When they got to her house, she led him up the walkway to the side gate. He asked again what they were doing and she responded with a finger pressed to her lips, and a whispered "Shhh."

Lisa opened the gate for them and they stepped into the yard. Her stepdad's truck was parked on the driveway, filling half the yard. Her mom's summer garden was in full glory, and in the moonlight looked to be a tangled mess of vines and leaves. The sweet smell of new tomatoes rode the breeze to meet them. Still holding Joe's hand, Lisa led him across the yard to the little shed.

Quietly, Joe asked "Where are you taking me?" It came out in a laugh. When Joe was happy, he spoke in laughter, his words bobbing up and down like a buoy bouncing in the water.

His hand was warm and enveloped hers with a solid assurance she'd never noticed before.

When she pushed the door open, she said, "Look."

Following her lead, Joe knelt down in the doorway. Kiwi opened her eyes for a mere second, before closing them again. Some of the kittens were nursing, pulling at their mother's teats and kneading with their impossibly tiny paws, and some of them were sleeping in a heap. Lisa counted heads again and whispered, "Six."

With their bodies squeezed together in the narrow doorway, she both felt and heard Joe exhale his awe. He looked at her with his dazzling smile and drank it all up like she knew he would. The kittens, the moonlight, the night air, the girl he thought he loved kneeling next to him; he was here for it all, and Lisa had somewhere to pour her joy.

They shared a smile, then looked back at the box of kittens.

"Wow," Joe whispered.

"Yeah," Lisa agreed.

nothing ever lasts forever

Izzy Thorpe

The silence hangs heavy between us. I've always been the type of person to say something, anything, to fill the space when it gets too quiet. This time though, I simply have nothing to say.

I want to say something but the words wilt past my lips and I only end up opening and closing my mouth like a fish out of water. Miles probably would have commented on that if he could see me, but he's too busy staring out the front windshield. It's started to rain and the yellow glow from the streetlights is refracting in the raindrops in a way that makes it hard to see. Miles is gripping the wheel tight, focused more on driving than on conversation. I don't think he knows what to say either.

I love you, I want to say. I want to say it until the words can rewind time until we're both back sitting at that restaurant, before Miles told me that we couldn't be together anymore. *I love you, I love you, I love you*. I'd say the words until things were different if it worked like that. I wanted the phrase to be magic, a spell that could turn '*I wish things could be different*,' into, '*I love you too*'. I'm sitting in the passenger seat of this goddam car with the love of my life driving home for probably the last time and I can't think of a single thing to say because the only thing I want to say is I love you. And I can't say that.

"So," Miles says at last, disrupting the silence, "do you think I can come by tomorrow and pick up my stuff?"

"*No*," I want to say like a petulant child, because if I still have a pair of his socks and a handful of the vintage records that he loves then he can't really be gone. The rational part of my brain knows that he'll still be leaving, with or without his stuff. Holding his stuff hostage would just end up hurting us both.

Instead, I say, "Sure, tomorrow works." Again, the silence falls between us.

"Are you mad?"

I say nothing.

"You know, I really tried to make this work."

"I know... I'm not mad, I'm just upset," I say because it's more appropriate for the situation than '*I love you*'.

"Yeah, I'm upset too," Miles mumbles. He still doesn't look at me, he keeps his eyes locked on the road. I wish I could hug him to make things better, but right now it just might make things worse.

The traffic light turns red and Miles slows to a stop. There's only the low thrum of the radio and the beating of the windshield wipers fighting against the drizzling rain.

Casually, Miles leans over and turns the knob on the radio until the music is blaring around us. I reach over to turn the music down, but Miles turns it back up louder than before. He rolls down the windows to let out some of the sound and we both soon become covered in a layer of fine mist.

The instrumental builds and I recognize the song instantly. It's one of Miles' favorites, he always was a fan of 80's pop rock.

"Welcome to your life!" Miles sings the lyrics as they start, turning to me and pretending to hold a microphone, like he had done so many times before.

"Seriously?" I say, trying to hold back a smile.

"There's no turning back!" The words come out more of a shout than a song, but Miles manages to be loud enough to compete with the radio. Miles by no means had a bad voice under normal circumstances, but he's so loud that it makes it hard for him to carry a tune. He sounds ridiculous. I can't help the full blown grin that sneaks onto my face.

"We will find you!" Miles pumps his free fist around as he sings.

It's late enough that there aren't many other cars on the road, but I still wonder if the apartment complex across the street can hear us. Handing me my own imaginary microphone, I can't imagine that Miles cares about that. I try to refuse, but he nudges his loosened fist towards me again.

"I know you know the words!" Miles shouts over the music.

I shake my head then snap up, "Turn your back on Mother Nature!" I've formed my own imaginary mic and am singing into it.

"Everybody wants to rule the world!" We shout the words together. Miles mimes a guitar to match the instrumentals and I add an imaginary keyboard to our impromptu band. The way I slam my fingers into the fake keys makes Miles laugh and I feel the tension between us melt.

"It's my own design... It's my own remorse..." we sing together, both out of tune and laughing between lines. The light has turned green and Miles drives forward filling more of the night air with our horrendous music. There's a sheen to our skin now from the rain, but neither of us care.

"Most of freedom and of pleasure, nothing ever lasts forever!" That line breaks my heart a little as I sing it. I wouldn't be feeling this way if some things could last forever. Even this moment between us would end.

"I'm so glad we've almost made it! So sad they had to fade it! Everybody wants to rule the world!"

We sing until it feels like it's just the two of us in the world, together against everything. Miles did the same thing on our first date driving to dinner, played the music too loud and sang until we laughed away the first-date awkwardness. We met in our sophomore lit class and for some reason we waited until the end of the semester to go on a date. If I knew this is how it would end, I would have run up on the first day and kissed him then and there so as not to waste a single second.

"Say that you'll never, never, never, never, need it!" I stop singing for a moment and look over at Miles, taking him in. I try to remember the way he looks right now, so that this happy, carefree face will be the one I see in my memories. The yellow street light gleams against his mist-covered skin making him look electric. He's beautiful, the man I love, and I want to remember that. He looks over at me and smiles a smile so goddamn perfect it melts my heart. It feels like my chest is going to explode, with either love or pain, I don't know. Maybe a mix of both.

"Everybody wants to rule the world!" We sing together, and it's perfect. We finish up the song, just as wild and out of tune as we started. Eventually, the next song on the radio starts to play and we just sit there with the blaring music between us. I'm the one who reaches over and turns the radio back to a normal volume.

"I love you, you know." Miles says, eyes fixed on the road.

I love you, I love you, I love you. "I know," I say because deep down, I'm a realist that knows as soon as Miles got that job offer on the other side of the country that we wouldn't make it. I knew that we would have to break up eventually, even if we spent weeks pretending otherwise. I want to hate him for leaving me, but I love him too much for that. I get it. As much as it hurts, I get it.

"Should I just say screw it? Tell the job that I'm not willing to relocate?" Miles asks, and I can tell by the tremor in his voice that there's no good answer I could give. We both want more than what's possible.

"You can't," I say at last, not bothering to explain why he can't give up on his dream for me. He doesn't push it. Ever since he was a kid, Miles has wanted to be a wildlife conservationist and help save the world. At last, an offer came in from the best nonprofit in the country. It also happened to be on the other side of the country.

He also doesn't ask me to go with him. I have my own dreams, a specific life that I want to build for myself. For a million and one reasons, I need to do that here. Miles knows this, we've talked the situation to death. I guess I've always known deep down that our relationship had a clock on it, but I couldn't help myself. After four years I wouldn't trade for anything, breaking up was the only solution either of us could come up with.

Miles doesn't make any grand promises like that we'll see each other again eventually or that maybe there's a chance we could do long distance. He just drops me off with a 'see you tomorrow' like it's any other day instead of one of the last few times we'll see each other.

"See you," I say walking away from the car. After I pause, I turn back and add, "I love you." He smiles at me then rolls the windows up before driving off. In my head, I can still see his beautiful smile. I can still hear him singing. *Nothing ever lasts forever.*

about the authors

ALLISON MATALONE

Allison is a stay at home mom who, when not getting puked on or picking up kids from school, likes to stare at a computer screen and occasionally put her thoughts down onto a document. She hopes to eventually produce something substantial.

Also she loves her husband, Daniel, and sons: Dominic, Vincent, and ~~TBD~~ Zachary.

AMANDA KENNEDY

Amanda combines her love of writing and her love of deep, soulful conversations in the two writing groups she leads with her writing friends. She credits her successes and growth as a writer to the beautiful people she gathers with regularly to sharpen their figurative pencils. Among the many books on writing, literary fiction, memoirs and Stephen King novels on her bookshelf, is Natalie Goldberg's Writing Down the Bones (1986), which has informed her writing style and approach to the craft since she first discovered it.

Amanda also teaches fitness classes, climbs mountains once in a while, and tries to keep up with her four kids. You can find her published works in the anthologies, Better Together (2023) and Just a Hint of Fantasy (2023). She's currently working on her first novel and planning a way to meet Natalie Goldberg.

BROOKE THOMPSON

Brooke Thompson has been writing since she was a little kid. She loves writing animal and fantasy stories. When she isn't writing, you can find her under a fuzzy blanket with her dog and a book.

CARISA H-K

Carisa H-K thrived for 25+ years in the technology sector before finding her higher calling. Drawing inspiration from the careers of Andy Weir and Daniel Suarez, she made a similar bold leap from the tech world to fiction writing. Carisa's debut work, **TALES FROM DIGITAL DELIRIA**, is an online short story collection that explores our digital age with bittersweet humor. This set the groundwork for her first novel, **FIGMENTS (THE RE-LIFE STORY: BOOK ONE)**, which is previewed in this collection. Leveraging her creative foundation from SMU Meadows School of the Arts and a unique perspective born from decades of web building, Carisa H-K's writing unearths the human stories trapped inside our technology-driven world. For more information about her forthcoming novel, stay connected at **www.CarisaHK.com**.

CHRISTINE URGELLO

Christine enjoys reading, gardening, yoga and poetry. Her favorite thing is curling up on the couch with hot tea and a whodunit on rainy days. She is devoted to her husband, three children and the NYT games. She does her best not to believe in astrology.

DAVID HANSEN

David Hansen is a storyteller, therapist, and sometimes writer and poet. He loves to listen to others and tell his stories in equal measure. His other roles include father, advocate, social justice learner, philosopher, psychonaut, spiritualist, and deconstructionist.

IZZY THORPE

Izzy Thorpe is a serial hobbyist. She enjoys painting, drawing, gardening, reading, and, of course, writing. That and curling up on the couch with her cat and a hot cup of tea. Izzy writes to share her perspective on the world and to share the wild stories that float through her head.

K.I. RUNYON

Karoline is a Type A corporate fiend who never knew that writing was the creative outlet she needed. Using her excel wizardry and her love for traveling and hiking, she tries to find a delicate balance between plotting scenes down to the exact word count and imagining brand new worlds. Her current work in progress is a fantasy novel, which she hopes to publish in the next few years. Karoline is married to a fantastic and wonderfully supportive human and is a devoted cat mom to Wallace and Bernie.

LEE GRAHAM

THE PROPHECY delves into the insidious nature of generational trauma, exploring how the cycle of abuse and unaddressed pain can shape the pursuit of truth and personal identity.

Lee Graham is a poet and fantasy author whose work has previously appeared in October Hill Magazine. With a deep fascination for folklore, Lee's writing explores the intersection of myth, reality, and human emotion. They hold degrees in Drama and Creative Writing from New York University, and are currently working on their debut poetry book.

ROSE PULFORD

Rose Pulford is a romance writer who brings a hint of comedy and sarcasm to her heartfelt love stories. By day, she works in marketing, but in her free time, she's writing with her dog curled up beside her and a Diet Coke close by. Starting with poetry, Rose has performed at poetry slams and won a haiku contest at UTD. Now, inspired by romcom authors like Emily Henry, she crafts complex character relationships with the goal of making her readers feel like they're watching a movie unfold. She's happily addicted to chocolate and dreaming up happily-ever-afters.

TARA HENDERSON

Tara's writing journey started in the second grade when she got a pink diary with lock and key for her eighth birthday. She never stopped journaling. In 2018 her writing practice evolved into actual work. Today she has three novel drafts, two NaNoWriMo wins, a blog, a parenting workbook, and a part-time job copy writing for various businesses. Her passion for building community and encouraging intentional living continues to drive her daily life. She is a California native currently residing in Dallas, TX with her husband, teenagers, a dog, a cat, and a calendar full of joy. She is currently working with The Book Incubator to turn one of her novel drafts into a published work.

editor's note

Tara Henderson

"Kindred spirits are not so scarce as I used
to think. It's splendid to find out there are so
many of them in the world."

– L.M. Montgomery, Anne of Green Gables

Stories attempt to capture the complicated web of human experiences, each highlighting a perspective unique to the narrator's journey. Before written words, stories were handed down verbally; their significance undiminished by the oft times ever-changing details. The first fish caught by a twelve-year old evolves from six inches to two feet long, hands growing wider and wider apart with each retelling. But the listeners don't see the need to correct it. The story is fun. It is flawed. It is the human experience.

Like stories, the connection that we make with another person is unique to us. We may never know the impact of a kind word, a ride home, or an invitation made until much later, if ever. In this year's anthology we wanted to capture the essence of what brought the Kindred Writing Collective together. Each story was read by our judges with the aim of filling the anthology with tales that reflect the multi-faceted adventure of relationships.

As each of us wrote our own pieces, we drew from our experiences and our imaginations, as writer's do for everything that they create. Members of the Kindred Writing Collective strive for authenticity in all of their work, as one should aspire to in one's personal life.

What started as an experiment in the local library has grown into eleven dedicated members, an annual anthology, and a writing fair. Producing good writing is an obvious aim of our collective, but in addition, we seek genuine connection. It is through these connections that we become better writers. Because, to write a good story, one that others will want to read, we must tap into those parts of humanity that resonate with universal truths and reveal our intrinsic needs for connection, purpose, and understanding. Stories allow all of that to happen in the safe space that lies between two covers (or maybe an ereader or audio book).

Publishing the anthology gives the Collective, and now other authors, a place to explore these themes, as well as genres and styles. Each anthology features a different focus with the purpose of challenging our writing practice and pushing ourselves out of our comfort zones. With that in mind, we present to you, "the hands we choose to hold," the second edition of the Kindred Writing Collective Anthology. We hope that you enjoy it!

To keep in touch and to learn about KWC events and opportunities, please follow us on Instagram @KindredWritingCollective